# Footsteps

by

Barnaby Newman

PublishNation
www.publishnation.co.uk

"And still man must question, must know, and with the questions come answers, and with the answers, the magic is lost."

# 1

Jeannie watched her friend leave the music shop, she was concerned for him, since his grandmother died, he seemed to be struggling even more to keep connected to the modern world around him.  There wasn't much she could do, other than to keep dragging him back into civilization.

She turned to see the shopkeeper, Tim, frowning at the door.

"I'm a little worried about your friend, David," he said.

"Why, what's up?" she asked.

"Well, I just asked him how he got on with that relaxation music you bought him last week.  He said he loved the CD, that it really helped him to relax, but he said the footsteps at the end were a bit too loud and out of place and freaked him out a bit," replied Tim.

"And?"

"Jeannie, I must have listened to that music a hundred times or more, there are no footsteps."


There is a small glade inside a deep dark wood, inside the glade is an old cottage, it has been there for many years and housed many generations.  It has sat there for a long time surrounded by the woodland.  The woodland has been there even longer.

Some say the woodland is haunted, although many people assume that of places that are old.  Some say it has been there so long that it spans back to a time when the old folk were still here, the creatures and spirits that many believe now exist purely in old folk tales, myths and legends.  Some say they are still there, in the darkest shadows, in the deepest heart of the forest.

Or maybe it is merely the wind through the trees, a trick of the mind, an imagining.  Either way, it has remained a quiet place, remote, in a landscape that has been changing around it.

David was the new owner now, after his grandmother passed away three years earlier. He was born in the cottage and had been raised there by his grandmother as his mother had died giving birth to him. He had never known who his father was. At twenty-two he now found himself in possession of his own home, alone in the woodland in which he had grown up. His grandmother had brought him up simply, they had enough land inside the glade to grow much of their own food and the woodland provided their heat, he had been taught that those were the most important things you needed. David knew every inch of the woods, he knew the different types of trees, all the flora and fauna that was taught to him by his grandmother, the woodland held no fears for him. The world outside the woods became the bigger challenge.

On his childhood days when the chores were done, he had the whole of the woods to run wild in, most days on his own but occasionally his school friends Marcus and his sister Jeannie would visit. Jeannie had been his friend for years, and her brother Marcus, but David didn't see Marcus much anymore. He had gone on to college and was now working in Southampton as an accountant, he had left the woods of their childhood far behind and no longer understood David's connection to them. Jeannie still understood the fascination with the natural world, she loved to visit and walk through the forest, even though she too had moved from the edge of the forest where she and Marcus had grown up and had settled in an apartment near the city where she worked in a large chain bookstore. David never fully understood how she could thrive in the city.

With the cottage left to him he had been able to concentrate on his main hobby, carving sculptures from wood. He was good at it and getting better all the time, he was now selling pieces out of an art studio in a small local town and the revenue was enough to pay the few bills that came in.  It meant that he spent longer and longer on his own at the cottage in the woodland, so Jeannie paid lots of visits and dragged him out to the local pubs when there was music on, trying to make sure he stayed connected to the world outside.

She had invited him into town again today, her friend who ran a music shop there had told her that the music David had ordered had arrived.  David always caught the train in rather than drive and then hunt for a parking space.  It was a four mile walk from his cottage to the train station, but he liked to walk, it helped to clear his mind.  He was finding it hard to switch off and still wasn't sleeping.  Jeannie had bought him some relaxation music a few weeks ago to try to help him, he had thought it a bit new age for his tastes, but she had insisted that he take it.

"Try the CD David, it may help you to sleep," she had said, smiling at him.  "Who knows, maybe it will open up a whole new world for you."

It was impossible to refuse Jeannie when she was in an upbeat mood and so he had taken the disc and it turned out she was right, it was very relaxing, flute and harp music with deep strings in the background and birdsong.  He wasn't sure if he had fallen asleep, he didn't think he had, but towards the end he had suddenly heard footsteps, hard leather soles on a cobbled street.  It was so different to the other noises on the track that it brought him straight out of his daze.  He had mentioned it to the shop owner when he was there last and got a strange look in return, but David thought it was a fair comment, there was nothing relaxing about hurried footsteps.

He got off the train in Southampton and headed for the park, he was meeting Jeannie in her lunch break and any day when it wasn't raining, she would take a pack lunch and find a bench out in the open air.  The music shop wasn't far from the park and the owner was a good friend of Jeannie's, she often popped in there for a quick coffee on her way back from the bookshop.

Jeannie was just finishing her sandwiches as David approached and she stood up and gave him a kiss on the cheek.

"Hi David, how's things? Have a nice walk across the forest? She asked.

"Yes, it's a lovely day for it. Some of the ponies are starting to have their young, so there are a few wobbly foals about." Replied David.

"I shall have to head out there with my camera at the weekend then," she said.

They headed out of the park, across the road and down one of the side streets to the little music shop. Tim had purchased the shop a couple of years ago and had decided to concentrate mainly on folk music, keeping tabs on some of the more obscure past and present music brought out. He had figured there was no point in selling exactly what the large stores were selling, and it had seemed to pay off, the shop had managed to gain plenty of loyal customers and in a time when a lot of the smaller shops were struggling, he was doing quite well.

"Hello, you two," he greeted them. "I will be with you in a moment, stick the kettle on back there if you like Jeannie."

She went back behind the counter and through the door that led to the storeroom, toilet, and small kitchenette. Tim finished serving his customer and reached down under his till to the shelving below.

"Those couple of cd's you ordered last time have arrived David, looks like some good stuff. There's electric in that cottage of yours then?" he asked grinning.

"Yeah, all the mod cons," replied David. "But it's all on a dynamo so I don't like to use it too much, wears the donkey out, you know?"

"Lot of effort for a light bulb and a bit of music," said Tim, nodding and chuckling.

Few people got David's sense of humor, but Tim seemed on the same wavelength and David liked him, he could see how Jeannie had become good friends with him. He sorted out the money for the discs as Jeannie came back through the door with the coffees.

"So, Jeannie tells me you're a sculptor?" said Tim, taking a sip. "What sort of stuff do you do?"

"Animals mainly, out of wood. A shop in Lymington sells them for me on commission. The tourists seem to like them," said David, shrugging.

"David is underselling himself," said Jeannie. "His work is really good."

"Does it pay well?" asked Tim.

"It covers the bills I get, keeps the wolves from the door."

"You will have to pop over and see him at work one day," said Jeannie.

David shot her a look.

"I'd like that," said Tim. "Listen you'll have to excuse me a second, I've got to water the horse."

He popped back through to the toilet. David stood looking at Jeannie.

"What?" she asked.

"You know what," he said lightly. "You invited him out to the cottage."

"At some point, yes, to see your work, you know it's good."

"And you know people's response to the cottage," he said chuckling. "They have a romantic idea of it in their head, then they turn up and stand there in the glade, they scratch their head, then they scratch their arse, then they make up some crap excuse about something they've forgotten to do, and then they disappear."

Jeannie was laughing.

"Tim's different," she said. "He likes you, and you need more friends than just me in this world David."

David nodded.

"Yeah well, maybe you're right, he seems ok."

Tim returned with a big box of discs and set it on the counter.

"Something to keep me busy this afternoon, always goes dead in here on a Wednesday afternoon, don't know why. Oh, and I was going to ask you two what you were up to Friday night? A cousin of mine is in a little folk trio and they are playing over your way David, in the Moonlight. I said I'd go along and give them a bit of support, thought I could pick you up Jeannie, and you David if you like?"

"I'm up for that," said Jeannie.

"Yeah, could do, I've not been across there in a while," said David. "I can walk it from mine though, it's only a mile and a half."

They turned to leave but Tim stopped them again.

"Oh, and David, I was meaning to ask, did you play that relaxation disc again?"

"Yes, a couple of nights ago."

"Were there still footsteps on it?"

"Yes, they almost seemed a little louder this time, a little closer," replied David. "Maybe I was just waiting for them."

"Maybe," said Tim nodding. "Any chance you could have fallen asleep?"

David shrugged.

"It's always possible. Didn't feel like I had, bit of a daydream perhaps, why?"

"I just wondered if it was something on the disc, that maybe you got a duff copy somehow. I tell you what, bring yours along Friday night and I'll dig out a fresh copy from the storeroom to swap it with and you can try another one."

"Ok, cheers," said David.

He walked Jeannie back to the bookshop, popping in himself to buy a couple of new books, and then headed back to the train station.

The Moonlight Tavern never got jam packed but there was usually a good crowd in there on a live music night. Tim and Jeannie were already there when David arrived just before eight o'clock and had found themselves a table by the wall to the left-hand side of the band, opposite the bar. Tim got up as he saw David enter and met him at the bar.

"My round David, what are you having?"

"Pint of best please," said David as the barman approached them.

"Two of those please," said Tim to the barman. "And a JD and coke as well please?"

"Jeannie's on the hard stuff tonight then, eh?" said David smiling.

"Yeah, hard day at the shop apparently. Glad you could make it."

"I used to pop in here regularly, especially when there was live music on, but not so much recently. I thought it might be good to get back out, Jeannie's always telling me I should get out more!"

Tim smiled at him.

"She thinks very highly of you, says you've known each other a long time?"

"Yeah, we grew up together, bit like a brother and sister I suppose. Looked after each other at school, not that she needed much looking after."

"No, she seems a tough one. We better get back to her I guess."

They made their way over to the table and sat down just as the band started up their first number. They turned out to be quite good and David was glad he had come along, the drinks were going down well too. As Tim was driving, he had switched to cokes, but David and Jeannie were into a bit of a session, and they were all having a laugh together while tapping their feet along to the band and joining in singing along to a few of the songs.  Towards the end of the first set a group of three young men came in and headed across to the bar, one of them nodded over to David and David nodded back.

"Oh great," he said.  "It's the jesters, I was hoping they wouldn't be in here tonight."

"The jesters?" asked Tim.

"Yeah, it's a nickname a few of the locals in here coined for them.  They tend to roll in here when there's music on and they get a bit silly, well, more than a bit sometimes.  Most of the locals in here like a drink and a bit of a laugh but it's a small pub, those three will be jigging and dosey doing by the end of the next set, by the last they will likely be knocking over chairs and spilling people's drinks.  They're harmless enough, I know one of them, Johnny, from years ago, but they can annoy some people and their antics have been known to kick start the odd fight.  The landlord won't chuck them out unless it gets truly out of hand because they put a lot of money across the bar," he shrugged, "I guess they liven it up a bit as well really, like I say, they're harmless enough.  Just keep an eye on what they're doing when you're on your way to the bar or the loo, if they're cavorting around, they're likely to knock you into somebody else and that's when the trouble can start."

"Thanks for the warning," said Tim.

By the end of the next set David's predictions were starting to come true and the three lads were starting to get quite rowdy.  The band had been creating a good lively atmosphere so there was plenty of people making a noise and having a little dance, but David knew the signs from those three.  He was planning to leave before the next set started but Tim had insisted it was his round and bought another drink and so David said he would stay for one more.

The last set was full of lively numbers, and everybody was enjoying themselves. David was glad he had stayed and was getting to know Tim a lot better, he could see why he and Jeannie got on so well, he seemed quite a humble man. The three of them were chatting away together when Johnny knocked into David mid reel and nearly spilled his pint down him.

"Sorry Davey mate," he said putting his hand on David's shoulder. "Can I get you a refill?"

"No, I barely spilled a drop Johnny, no harm done."

"Well, sorry all the same. It's good to see you back in here David," replied Johnny wobbling slightly. "It's good to see you're doing ok," he patted David's shoulder and looked across the table at the others. "Sorry David's friends," he said smiling. "Enjoy your evening, I shall take my leave."

With that he did a comical theatrical bow, bumping into the man behind him as he did it and spilling half the man's drink down him.

"Here we go," muttered David.

The man immediately got irate at Johnny, swearing at him and grabbing Johnny by his shirt collar. Johnny was waving his palms at him apologizing and offering to replace the man's drink, but the man was just showing anger.

David looked across the table at Jeannie and rolled his eyes. He put his pint down and stood up, turning to face the two men.

"There's no need for that fella," he said to the man still holding Johnny by the scruff of the neck. "He's offered to buy you a replacement and he's apologized."

"After chucking half my drink down me."

"Ah well, it happens, he damn near did the same to me. The lads here work hard for their money, and it's a thumping good band, the boys are just letting off steam. No harm done."

"Not to you maybe. Who are you anyway, his boyfriend?"

"Just a local out enjoying a pint and some good music. I think it's time you let everybody get back to enjoying their evening, and I think Johnny here is slowly turning blue," he said trying to keep things light. "How about you let him go?"

With that David moved to detach Johnny from the man's grasp, at which point the man turned on David instead, taking a swing at him. David had been prepared for such a move and dodged nimbly out of the way, using the man's momentum to keep him turning whilst moving the man's arm up behind his back. Keeping him in that position he caught the landlord's eye and nodded to him as he continued to escort the man out of the pub. Tim appeared at his elbow and opened the door for him allowing him easier access and they persuaded the man down the steps and into the carpark, both withdrawing back up the steps straight away so as not to be threatening. The landlord appeared at the top of the steps just as the man was heading back towards them.

"One more step and you're barred for life," said the landlord. "I don't want that kind of behavior in my pub, and there's no other pub for three miles, your choice."

The man wavered with one foot on the bottom step then obviously thought better of it and headed off out of the carpark.

"Thanks for that David. Not seen you for a long time, how come you stopped coming in?"

"I grew tired of playing an unpaid doorman!" David replied, looking sideways at the landlord and smiling.

The landlord laughed.

"Well, I'd best get you a pint on the house then!"

"Not for me thanks Neil, I planned to just finish the one I'm on and head off. I think I'll stick to that plan in case that chap comes back with some friends."

"I doubt he's got many of those," replied Neil opening the door for them.

"Who is he anyway? Does he live round here?" David asked.

"He's bought one of the thatch cottages along the main road. As the older generation passes on the money crowd are moving in."

"Good for business?" asked Tim.

"No doubt, if you want to run a posh restaurant but I never got into this game for that. A bunch of stiffs sitting around in candle-light? They can go into town for that sort of thing. A proper little country boozer is what I wanted," he laughed and nodded over to Johnny and his friends who were now dosey doing to another lively tune while over half of the locals were clapping in time. "And that's what we've got. Are you sure I can't tempt you to that free drink David?"

David shook his head.

"Some other time perhaps Neil. Thanks though, it's been a good evening, great band."

The landlord gently clapped him on the shoulder and went back around behind the bar. David and Tim went back to their table to rejoin Jeannie, but David didn't bother to sit down, instead he picked up the last of his pint and drained it.

"Well, that's enough fun for me for one night, I'm off."

"Can I give you a lift?" asked Tim.

"No that's ok, it's much shorter to walk it than drive it, I can cut through the forest."

"You're mad walking through there in the pitch black!"

"Why? I know it too well to get lost, lover boy back there won't be hanging around he'll be tucked up nice and warm in his thatch with some brandy by now and there's nothing in the forest to be frightened of."

Tim nodded, chuckling.

"Well, ok, but I don't think I'd fancy it much. Take care David, it's been good to finally spend some time with you."

"You too," said David.

He gave Jeannie a hug goodbye and left them to the music and the noise of the pub.

As he had predicted, his walk home was uneventful, but the confrontation in the pub had left him a little unsettled. It was the first time he had been out for a while, and he had already got himself into an awkward position. People kept telling him he had to mix but whenever he did this kind of thing always seemed to happen. He could have stayed out of it of course and let them fight it out but it had always been his nature to try and calm things down and look after those he knew, and Johnny had always been a mate, it wouldn't have felt right to just stand back and do nothing.

It was all still going around inside his head when he arrived back at his cottage and so to try and make sure he got a good night's sleep he decided to put on the fresh cd that Tim had given him at the pub. He had a couple of sculptures that he wanted to have a go at finishing the next day, so he wanted a restful night. He flaked out on the sofa and put the music on, and let the relaxing strings and birdsong carry him away.

Drifting, floating, carried along with the music, he sank into a deep calm. He was warm and comfortable he could feel a gentle breeze on his face. Feel, he thought, yes that is strange, it's as if I can feel the breeze. And the warmth he could feel did not feel like that of the inside of his cottage, but more like the warmth of the sun. There were other things too. The smell of roses, the faint noises of a village waking up. How were his senses picking up these things so vividly? Too real to be a dream, too strange to be real.

Then, as before, he could hear footsteps. Light but hurried, on a cobbled street. You must stay with it, he told himself, you must find out what these noises are. He opened his eyes and found himself in a sun draped courtyard. To the left of the seat on which he sat was a bed of heavily scented pink roses, to the right was a corner of the courtyard with a high stone wall that looked like it led off down a small street, it was from that direction that the footsteps appeared to be coming from. In front of him across the courtyard there was just a low wall, tall enough that seated he could just see over it. All the stone was a pale grey, not one that he could recognize, certainly not one that he could place locally to his home. To the far left beyond the roses was a large opening in the courtyard wall where there stood open two large metal gates. The crafting of the gates was exquisite. On one was the shape of a big cat, on the other was a bear, so that they would face each other when the gates were closed. Through the gates was a wide track sweeping through beautifully landscaped grounds towards what looked like a small castle. This is nothing like anywhere I've ever been before, thought David, and then, as you will in a dream sometimes when you find yourself in surroundings you cannot place, he panicked. He suddenly stood up and took a stride forward to try and gain his bearings in a landscape totally alien to him. And as he stood up, stepped forward, and stood still again looking desperately around him for a landmark he could recognize, the owner of the footsteps turned the corner from the street into the courtyard and cannoned straight into him.

# 2

David somehow managed to save the tray, and most of the bread that was on it, but this didn't leave any free hands to save the young woman from sprawling across the gravel of the courtyard.  He had a moment of inaction before setting the tray down on the seat and turning once more to help the woman up.  As she got to her feet, she straightened out the long, pleated skirt she was wearing before looking up at David and gently removing his hand from her arm from where he had helped her up.

"Thank you," she said.  "I'm ok now."

"Sorry about that, are you alright?  Are you hurt?" David asked.

"I may have left some skin behind on the gravel," she replied, studying a graze on her lower palm and wrist.  "But no harm done."

"I really am sorry," said David.

She shook her head.

"It was my own fault, blundering around a blind corner like that.  I'm afraid I was in a bit of a rush.  I have got to get the bread up to the big house."  She looked across at the tray.  "I should thank you for saving the bread, I wouldn't have been too popular if I'd have thrown that all across the courtyard."

"I'm sure there's plenty of crows that would have thanked you."

"You're probably right there!" she said chuckling.

David was watching her while she laughed, he was mesmerized by her.  A little shorter than him, she had chestnut brown hair tied up in a ponytail that shone like polished wood in the morning sun.  The eyes that met David's were a deep green, piercing but warm, and touched with humor.  It had been a long time since he had met a girl who caught and held his attention so, and he stood there for a moment just watching her.

She was the first to break eye contact and lowered her gaze to fuss with her skirt again, brushing it down with her hands to make sure it was clean of any debris.

"So why were you standing in the middle of the path so early in the morning?" she asked, still checking her skirt.

"I was trying to get my bearings, I'm not sure where I am."

"You are in the entrance courtyard of the house of Selaster," she replied frowning a little. "You are not from around here then?"

David shook his head.

"Wherever here is," he added.

She looked at him again with a quizzical look.

"The world?" she said with a slight chuckle. "On the island lands of Larquolyn?"

"Sorry, I really don't know where I am," he said, feeling like he should try to explain. "I just somehow woke up on that bench there."

Her look changed to one slightly disapproving and she headed past him to where her bread had been left.

"Must have been some night," she said levelly.

"What?... No, I wasn't drunk if that's what you're thinking?... "Well, I'd had a couple, but... No, I fell asleep somewhere else, and I woke up here."

There's really no way I can explain this to anybody else, he thought, if it doesn't even make any sense to me. It wasn't a dream; he was almost sure of that. No kind of dream he'd ever had before anyway. He could feel everything, the gravel under his feet, the bruise developing on his arm where the tray had hit him. He could smell the roses, and the girl's light perfume.

"Well, you don't have to explain yourself to me," she said politely. "I really must get this bread up to the house."

He watched her walk off with the tray.

"Wait!" he called. "What's your name?"

She took several more steps and then called over her shoulder. "Anna".

"I'm David," he called back, but she was already heading through the open gates, and he wasn't sure if she had heard him.

After she had gone, he turned to look around at the rest of the courtyard, and it was then he realized he could see the sea over the low wall. He walked over to the wall and looked down. The courtyard he was in was high up on a clifftop, down below was a natural harbor bustling with people and carts. Carts, thought David, not vans, not lorries, but carts. And then his eyes were drawn to the ships and boats that the goods were being unloaded from and loaded onto, and another moment of panic set in. Big wooden ships with tall masts and rigging, the kind that hadn't been used in David's world for centuries.

"Just where on God's earth am I?" he asked himself out loud.

He leaned on the wall for a few minutes looking out to sea while the hammering in his chest subsided and he could start to think straight. He knew it wasn't a dream. He could feel the stone of the wall, he could smell the sea, and he could feel the sun and wind on his face. He was here, wherever here was. But if it wasn't a dream then nothing else made sense. How do you get transported somewhere else?

David started to calm down and think. I'm not achieving anything just standing here, he thought to himself, I could wait for the girl to come back out and ask her some more questions, but I think I've held her up enough today, and I'm going to end up sounding weird. He decided to head down to the town and try to get some clues as to what was going on.

The town was like stepping back in time. The streets were cobbled, there were no cars, and most of the wares that the shops were selling were simple things, the goods that people needed daily to live their lives. There were bakers and butchers, a blacksmiths, tailors, and haberdashery. No phone shops, no large chain takeaways, no beauty salons. Even the folk from the small town near to where David lived would consider this the backwoods, but David was enjoying it. It was a busy bustling town and yet there was a quietness to it that appealed to him. He listened to the simple conversations between the people on the street and the shop owners and their customers as he passed by. As David walked a little further downhill he came to a pub, the sign above the door read The Bear Tavern, and behind the tavern there was what looked like a woodyard. Inside the woodyard was a large man of around fifty talking loudly and animatedly to another man of around the same age who was sat on a pile of logs. The man sitting down looked a little worse for wear. David couldn't help himself and moved closer to listen to their conversation.

"I don't know what to do with you," the big man was saying. "I really don't. I keep trying to help you, but you won't help yourself! What would you do in my place?"

The thinner man sitting down just shrugged and continued to look at his feet.

"I've got the tavern to run, I've got the woodyard to organize, I've got customers who depend on me who will go elsewhere if they get bad service here, I can't afford to be a charity Vrin, it's my livelihood too!"

The seated man nodded, "I understand," he said quietly.

"I gave you fair warning Vrin, more than once, I'm going to have to find somebody else. It's bad enough that I was out here at dawn chopping the wood when you should have already been here, but what am I to do now? You're in no fit state to deliver it and I have to be here to oversee the tavern, I can't be traipsing around town with the cart!"

He turned to point at the cart and in so doing he spotted David for the first time standing just outside the gates. At first, he scowled at the intruder who was stood listening to his conversation, but then his face relaxed and he called amicably enough across to David.

"And who might you be eavesdropping on our chat?"

"Sorry, I heard a raised voice, I wasn't sure where it was coming from. I'm new in town, still trying to get my bearings." Said David, hoping he hadn't offended this tank of a man.

The man nodded. "Well, no harm done then I guess. This fellow here that I'm shouting at is my late wife's cousin, Vrin. In respect to her I gave him a job a while back, to cut and chop the deliveries of wood that come into the yard here and then to take the pony and cart around the town and deliver the wood to the customers. But Vrin here likes a drink. So, some mornings he turns up here barely fit enough to do the work, and some mornings, like this morning, he doesn't damn well turn up at all!" The big man bellowed, looking back at Vrin. "He's been told enough times, no, to tell the truth he's been told too many times, and now I'm going to have to find a replacement." He stood rubbing his chin in thought while looking David up and down. "New in town you say? Going to need a job then. Can you chop wood? Know anything about horses, can you lead a pony and cart?"

"Yes" David replied.

"Want a job?"

David didn't know what to say. He felt sorry for the chap sitting on the log pile, but he could also sympathize with the innkeeper. His belly was already starting to rumble, and although it seemed crazy seeking employment here in this world, he was aware he couldn't eat fresh air.

The innkeeper was watching David look from himself to Vrin and could see the indecision on David's face.

"Listen, if you're worried about stepping on another man's toes you don't have to worry, I'll see Vrin's alright. He's my wife's cousin and I won't see him out on the street. He can have a bed made up out in the barn and I'll see he's fed, but rooms are for paying guests and workers."

Vrin looked up at David.

"Take the job son, it's a good job. Everything he says is true, he needs somebody reliable and reliable is one thing I'm not. I've abused his trust and generosity long enough." He looked at the innkeeper. "Although, I would appreciate a corner in the barn on cold nights cousin."

He levered himself off the wood pile and went to shake the innkeeper's hand, as he did so David saw the big man slip something into Vrin's hand and pat him on the shoulder. The thin man pocketed the item and gave David a nod on passing as he weaved his way out of the yard.

The landlord introduced himself to David as Azron. He explained to David that there wasn't much time as the cart should have left some time ago, but he would show David around later after he had finished the round.

David instantly liked the landlord. He was a large, gruff, formidable character, but he seemed fair and genuine. They put the pony in harness together and loaded the split logs onto the cart.

"So where are you from?" asked Azron. "The western lands by the looks of you."

David just nodded. It was probably best to let people come to their own decisions about him.

"What work did you do back home then?"

"Woodsman." David replied.

"Aye?" Well, maybe a bad day won't turn out so bad after all then. Spent much time around ponies?"

David ran his hand through the chestnut mare's mane and patted her neck.

"Yes, I know ponies."

"Well, this one shouldn't be any trouble," said Azron relaxing. "You have to make several trips out each day, she can't haul it all in one go and no point in trying to do it with more than one horse as the streets get narrow in places. We're about halfway up, or halfway down, depending which way you look at it, so when you turn left out of here to head uphill you deliver to the closest properties first, right? That way, the further she goes uphill the lighter her load becomes. No point in hauling a full cart all the way to the top."

"I'm not going to know where any of these addresses are to start with," said David.

"That's ok, I'll sort you out an order list and I'll draw you a map to get you started, there's bound to be people around you can ask if you get stuck. You get half a silver piece for each two days work, which you'll find is plenty for around here, unless you have a major thirst, in which case no amount of money will ever be enough," he said looking out through the gates and shaking his head sadly. "You get some breakfast and water in the morning, and an evening meal and a tankard of ale when you're done. Any drink you want after that is from your pocket, not mine. If you get hungry during the day you can buy something from the bakers. When you're done after your last delivery, you feed, water, and stable the horse and see she's alright for the night, then you come into the tavern, and we'll sort you out some food. Now I'll go and get your list and map and you can get on your way. Have you eaten this morning?"

David shook his head.

"I'll sort you something to take with you then, empty stomach's no good, the work is hard enough."

The work was hard enough. The pony was willing, but the streets got very steep in places, and here and there where it got busy with people there was quite a lot of stopping and starting which lost their momentum. David found that when he got to some of the houses the lack of access meant that he was carrying logs quite a distance on trips backwards and forwards from the cart. He was happy to be doing physical work though, and the customers he met were friendly.

On his trip back up from the harbor he came across a board with a picture of a map on it. The map was of a large island, the island of Larquolyn. On the southern tip of the map was the town of Selaster, so he guessed that was where he must be. Just up from the town was the edge of a huge forest that ran the length and breadth of the land. There were other towns out to the east and to the west, but the north looked empty. The towns out to the west were where the landlord had thought David was from.

As he stood there looking at the map, a short thin man stepped up beside him and joined him in studying the board.

"Are you lost?" asked the man.

"No," replied David. "I was just seeing how far I am from home."

The man nodded. "A long way from Mizule," he said, looking David up and down. "I'd guess that's where you're from. I travel a lot, see a lot of people."

"Mizule," said David, hunting it down on the map. "Yes, it is a long way."

"Well, that's the thing with a harbor town, you get a lot of different people from all over who turn up here."

The man smiled at David and went on his way. David took hold of the pony and started to lead her back up the hill. The day's work was finished, and David was looking forward to his meal after he had stabled the horse. Mizule…it was as good a place as any, and he had to have an answer ready if people asked where he was from.

His working day was due to start early, but it also finished quite early, so the tavern was reasonably quiet when he first set foot inside. The landlord greeted him cheerfully and found him a place to sit. He asked David how his first day had gone and then said he would give the kitchen a shout while he went to get his ale.

"There you go," said Azron, setting the tankard down in front of him.  "The food is just coming."

He slid a small silver coin along the table to David.

"One half silver piece," he said.  "I'll give you that for today to get you started.  It's kind of paying you double but you got me out of a hole this morning, and as you took the job there and then I'm guessing you don't have a penny in your pocket."

"Thank you," said David taking the coin.

"Don't spend it all at once, you won't get any more for two days."  Azron looked over to his right, "Ah, here comes your food, and here's somebody you should meet," he said with a smile as he stepped back from the table to allow the waitress to put the food down.

"Hello Anna," said David looking up.

"Hello David," she replied after a moment's pause. "Your food."

She turned and left again, leaving Azron standing there with his mouth open looking from David to Anna's retreating form and back again.

"You've met?" he asked David eventually.

"This morning," said David already tucking into the sausage, mash, and onion gravy that had been placed before him.

"You've only been in town one day and you're already on first name terms with Anna?"

David nodded.  "But I'm not sure she likes me much."

"Oh, she's a prickly one that one. Nice, but prickly. But you've got further in a day than most men get in weeks," said Azron laughing.  "You've had a very busy and productive day, lad, I'll leave you to enjoy your meal."

He wandered off back to the bar still chuckling to himself and David continued to devour his plate of food. In the end, David stayed at his table for a couple more tankards, enjoying the rest after the days work, and watching the tavern slowly fill up with the evening customers.  He could see that his half silver piece, although a fair wage, was not going to pay for a hefty, regular bar tab, but that suited him alright.  He was aware that unless he wanted to live in the same clothes each day, he was going to have to keep some money back to kit himself out over the next couple of days.  Finishing the last of his ale he headed to the bar and got Azron's attention.

"You mentioned a room for me to stay in the tavern?" said David.

"Yes, certainly.  The workers rooms are only small, but they are comfortable enough, hold on," Azron gave a customer their change and then called through the kitchen door behind him, "Anna."  A few seconds later Anna appeared at the door.

"Anna, sorry, I'm rushed off my feet behind the bar, could you please show David to his room?  It's room twelve," said Azron whilst filling another tankard.

"Of course," said Anna.  She turned to David.  "If you want to grab your pack and follow me, I'll show you where it is."

David started to follow her as she led him around the side of the bar to a staircase.  She glanced back and saw that he had no pack.

"You really did arrive in town on the hop," she said.

"Yes, I shall have to sort myself out some clothes."

"Well, there's a hardware shop down on Short Street that sells working clothes, and a not too posh tailors that should be within your budget in Market Place, if you want something a bit smarter.  You've done well to get a job here, Azron is not a bad person to work for."

"No, he seems alright," said David.  "So, do you do the two jobs permanently?"

"Yes. The work at the bakers is just the mornings, so then I work here later in the day to make up a wage. I live above the bakers, it's quieter than here."

"So, there's no husband? You live on your own?"

"There is nobody else," she said levelly.

"I'm sorry, I didn't mean to pry."

"It doesn't matter."

"Listen," said David. "About this morning. I wasn't hungover, I hadn't slept all night on that bench."

"It's ok, it really doesn't matter."

"It does to me. I wouldn't want you thinking that of me. It's just…well, it's hard to explain."

"Well, I have a huge pile of pots waiting to be washed up, so don't start explaining now. This is your room here," she said stopping at the end of the corridor.

"What time do you finish?" he asked.

She looked up at him and he could see it in her eyes, the connection he felt with her reflected back, whether she was willing to admit it or not.

"In about an hour."

"May I walk you back home?"

She looked at him again, looking him straight in the eyes. Whether weighing him up or weighing up her own decisions, he wasn't sure.

"You may," she eventually replied.

# 3

He walked her back home that night, and almost every night thereafter, returning home to the tavern after seeing her safely to her door.  He had been in Selaster now for almost three months, and life there suited him well.  He had proven himself more than capable at his job and had started to make friends around the town, including down at the harbor.  Occasionally on a day off he would go out fishing with a friend on their boat, or he would lend a hand to another on something that needed doing on their house.  He was starting to get known around the town.

His time spent with Anna was special to him, although they were both busy with their jobs, they found time to spend together, walking in the hills on the edge of town, sometimes taking a picnic with them.  But things could be difficult between them when the conversation got serious, when they started to discuss their future, when they started to question their past.  David found it impossible to explain that he had just turned up from somewhere else, somewhere else not even from this world, it made it seem like he was hiding something.  This in turn seemed to make Anna keep a distance between them, it was clear how they both felt but she refused to let them get any closer.  It had led to some rows between them, and days when they barely acknowledged each other at work.  David was aware that this caused nudges and amusement in the tavern between the customers and on occasions, Azron himself.  But David didn't care about them having their jokes, he just wanted himself and Anna to get things straight so they could be together, even if it meant somehow trying to explain how he got there.

After one particularly bad row, when they hadn't spoken to each other properly for several days, David waited for her to bring him his meal after work and slipped something into the pocket of her apron.  Anna assumed it was a note and paid no attention while she was busy at work.  She had forgotten all about it by the time she left, and it was much later in the evening when she suddenly remembered that he had put something in there.  When she went to her apron and put her hand in the pocket what she withdrew took her breath away.  It was a small carving of a running horse.  The detail carved into it was incredible and it was one of the most beautiful things she had ever seen.  The following day when David finished work and was stabling the pony, she had gone out to the stables to meet him before he headed into the tavern.

"The carving is beautiful David, thank you," she said.

"I'm glad you like it," he replied.  "It would've been quite a few hours wasted if you hadn't."

She stood there open mouthed.

"You mean you made that?  I thought you bought it!  You carved the horse yourself?"

He nodded and kept on brushing the pony.  "I just wanted to make a gesture.  I want things to be right between us."

Anna realized just how many hours he must have spent on the carving, and it diffused any existing argument between them.  She eventually took the brush from his hand and put her arms around him, holding on to him tightly.  Since then, things had been better between them, and David decided that they needed to find time to talk things through properly.

He asked Azron to give them both a few days off together and borrowed a couple of ponies from a friend on the outskirts of town so that he and Anna could go out riding and head out a little further into the hills.  He hoped that a change of scenery would do them both good.  They stopped by a river for a picnic and laid out on the blanket in the sun for a while, both enjoying the rest from their usual chores.

After some time, David sat up, watching the water flow by on down the valley.

"I can see it in your eyes, you know, every time we are together," said David. "You feel the same way, but every time we get close you withdraw, and you won't tell me why."

"I could say the same," said Anna, sitting up beside him. "We have known each other for months and yet I know nothing about you. You say you are from Mizule, but nothing about how you got here, and even what you do say doesn't seem to be the truth. I'm not saying I don't trust you, but I have my reasons to be careful, and reasons to not let people get too close."

Anna was gazing out across the valley and the river, deep in thought. Eventually she sighed and turned back to David.

"If I tell you, it can go no further. Nobody else is to know."

"Of course," said David. "I just need to know why you keep pushing me away."

"Because the last man I fell in love with was killed."

David looked at her wide eyed.

"How?" he asked.

"Protecting me."

David waited for her to go on.

"I used to work for the royal family in the east. When the queen was a young princess, I was her maid. She was five years older than me. I was twenty, she was twenty-five. We got on very well and became friends as much as anything else. But as she grew older, naturally she started to age, unnaturally, I didn't. When she became queen just over five years ago, she started to resent me. Rumors started flying around court that I must be a witch. The man I was with was one of her guards, he heard information that suggested I wasn't going to be safe much longer and decided to help me get away. I escaped, but he was killed in the process, and I have been moving every year since to try to stay clear of the queen and her guards. The minute she finds out I am here she will be after me, and anybody who is seen with me is in danger."

"But people age at different rates," said David. "I know some people don't deal with ageing well, but that's taking it to the extreme."

Anna locked eyes with David, so she had his full attention.

"David, it was twenty years ago I started working there. Do I look forty to you?"

He looked at her face as the information sank in. Unblemished, youthful, beautiful, she didn't look a day over twenty. He shook his head.

"The queen's outriders have turned up in every town I've lived in so far, they travel the entire land like they own it. They will turn up here and I will have to move on, I'm a fugitive. I can't expect anybody to tow along with me and anybody who does is in constant danger."

"But surely that is their own decision. At least I know the risks now. If I choose to be with you and I get hurt that's up to me."

Anna looked away, gazing over the valley once again.

"But there's a difference this time. The feelings I have for you are much stronger, the fear of getting close to you and then…I'm not sure I could cope if the same happened to you…if I lost you."

Her voice broke as the last few words were spoken, and the tears began to silently fall. David put his arms around her, and they sat there quietly again for a while. Finally, Anna detached herself from David and dried her eyes.

"I think I needed that," she said. "Just to release the pressure. One day I've wanted you, the next I've wanted to run, I haven't really known which way I was heading." She turned to David. "So now you know all about me, you know what you're taking on, and I need to know all about you. I know you're not from Mizule no matter what you may say. There's no real conviction when you say it, it's in your eyes, you don't believe it yourself."

"I'm not from Mizule, I'm not from this world at all, I'm from someplace else."

She sat looking at him, a slight frown developing on her face.

"Ok," she said.

"That day when you walked into me in the courtyard I had been listening to some music, sitting in a chair, and I had drifted off and woken up on that bench. I live in a little cottage in a forest, I sculpt things out of wood for a living, and I don't know what I'm doing here or where here is in relation to my own world."

Anna had her mouth slightly open now, as if she was about to ask a question but couldn't think which to ask first.

"Don't get me wrong," David continued. "My world is a lot different, but it's not necessarily better. I think I prefer it here, I fit in better here, and I've met nobody like you in my world. I don't want to go back, and I wouldn't even know how to."

Anna could see it wasn't a lie. It didn't make any sense, but what he was saying was clearly the truth. That truth came with other questions, other questions that she didn't really want to ask.

"What happens David, if you get pulled back to your own world and you can't get back here? What happens to me then? Do I become the mad old lady living as a recluse, waiting for her long, lost love to return? How do I carry on here not knowing if you are going to return or not?"

"I have no wish to go back."

"But you don't know how you got here, or why. So how can you know how long you will be here?"

David shrugged.

"That's true, but it also means that for all I know I could be here forever. I don't want to spend forever here without you."

Anna sat quietly for a moment, deep in thought. Eventually she slipped her arm through David's and took hold of his hand.

"Well, I've spent the last five years taking each day as it comes, I don't suppose a little longer will make much difference."

They spent the rest of the day together, talking and getting to know each other properly. The hills were quiet as they rode along enjoying the sunshine and the views of the valley. They saw a group of riders in the distance at one stage but did not come across them again, and they saw nobody else to interrupt their time together.

It was getting late when they returned to town, the market had packed down and the shops were all closed, most of the people were either at home or in the taverns and so the streets were quiet. They dropped the ponies back at the stables and walked the rest of the way back through the town. Once again, as he had so many times, David walked Anna back home. They stopped in the doorway of the bakers below the room where she stayed and embraced and kissed as they often had before. But when David finally detached himself and wished her goodnight, on this night Anna said nothing. She turned quietly and let herself through the door, leaving the door open behind her.

David woke to a sweet melody. He slowly opened his eyes and propping himself up on one elbow, looked around the room. In the corner of the room to the right of the window was a dressing table and mirror, sitting at the dressing table was Anna. She had her back to the bed and was gently brushing her hair in front of the mirror, she was in her own little world and was singing to herself.

"We will embrace.

And the fighting will cease.

The wars will all end

And the land will know peace.
Winter will pass.
With the sweet smell of spring
On the day when cometh the king."

David smiled and relaxed back onto the pillow watching Anna and listening to her as she sang another couple of verses, until she glanced down to the corner of the mirror and realized she had an audience. She smiled, a little embarrassed, and stopped singing.

"It's a beautiful song," said David.

"It's a song of hope. It's been passed down through generations for centuries apparently."

"I've heard the tune before."

"Really? When?" she asked.

David cast his mind back.

"On the day I left my world and turned up here." A frown crossed his face. "It was the tune playing in my cottage, but, how…?"

Anna turned around on her stool to face him.

"Well," she said. "I shall definitely stop singing it then." She playfully climbed onto the bed on her hands and knees and started crawling towards him. "I don't want you going anywhere."

As her face drew level with David's there was a knock at the door. Their eyes locked, and David could see Anna tense up, all joy and mischief gone from her face in a single second. Five years of running, five years of being alone with her fears, poised, ready to run again. She stepped back onto the floor at the side of the bed furthest from the door.

"Who is it?" she asked sternly.

"It's Azron, sorry to disturb you so early, and you David," he said with a slight chuckle. "But this is important."

Anna sighed and looked down at David forlornly.

"This cannot be good," she whispered.

She crossed the room and putting on her dressing gown she took a deep breath and opened the door.

"Azron, hello, please come in."

"Hello Anna," he said, stepping into the room. He looked at David sitting up in bed and raising one eyebrow he dipped his head. "David, good morning."

"It was," said David lightly. "But I fear that's about to change."

"Yes, very possibly I'm afraid."

"What is it?" asked Anna.

"I had a visit from Vrin this morning, very early. He said he was drinking with some friends in the Lion last night and heard somebody on a table behind him asking after you, or who he assumed was you. When the man had gone, Vrin turned to the people on the table and asked who the man was. The locals said they had never seen him before, they said he had been free with his money, so they sat and had a drink with him. When Vrin asked where he was from, they shrugged and said he sounded eastern and had the way of a soldier about him."

"I remembered you saying to me a while back that if anybody from the east turned up looking for you, to let you know, I never thought it would be a soldier. Are you in some sort of trouble?"

Anna nodded. "A little."

"Well, I thought I had better get over here at first light and let you know anyway. I like to keep tabs on what's happening in this town, so Vrin keeps an eye and an ear out for me, and I have others around town who do the same. It's good for business to know who's coming and going and if anything is happening that's going to affect profits. Anyway, there's a lad down at the harbor who works on the boats helping to load and unload goods, he caught me on my way here this morning and said several people coming down to the harbor yesterday said they had seen a dozen outriders from the east on the outskirts of town. It seems our friend in the pub last night may have some company with him."

"I bet that was the riders we saw yesterday," said David.

Anna nodded and sighed.

"It's time for me to move on Azron," she said, tears welling up in her eyes. "You've been so good to me, I've enjoyed living in this town so much, but if I stay here now, they will find me soon enough. Maybe there will come a day when I'm safe again and can return, but for now, I need to leave, and fast."

"I thought you would say that, so I've made preparations," said Azron. "There are two horses, bought and paid for, waiting in the stables behind my tavern, with provisions to last you a few days. I can't afford to buy you a sea voyage, you know how much they charge, so this is the best I can do. You'll have to go across country, through the forest I would say."

"But the forest is meant to be haunted," said Anna.

"Aye, meant to be, but people do travel through. It's dangerous enough I guess, but then so is open ground with a dozen soldiers on your tail."

"Aren't we likely to get lost in the forest?" asked David. "I'm used to the woods, but not this one."

"That's been accounted for. There is a guide I know who turns up in town now and then, he sees people safely through the forest in return for food and a reasonable payment. He's trustworthy, and he's been floating around town a while now, so I figured he didn't have any customers right now. I've sent an errand boy to where I know he is staying, with enough coin to tempt him, he should be waiting for you in the stables by the time you get there."

"Azron, how can we ever repay you?" asked Anna.

"You can't," replied Azron gruffly, "I'm about to lose my best timberman and waitress into the bargain as well, but you need to get gone. Come on boy," he said to David, "fun's over, get yourselves dressed and over to the stables, I'll meet you there."

When they got there, they found the horses saddled and packed with provisions, and the guide waiting for them as Azron had said he would be. The guide seemed familiar to David, but he couldn't place from where, just another face around town no doubt. Azron introduced the man as Shaeglin and saw them on their way. They turned left out of the timber yard, away from the harbor and uphill to make their way out of town. Before getting to the top of the hill they were to turn right into the marketplace where the stall holders would be setting up, and then continue through the streets from there out into the countryside, but before they got as far as the market from the top of the hill towards them came a group of four outriders. There was no point in them trying to turn and run from the riders as the only place they could run to would be down to the harbor and they would be trapped in a dead end, and so they sped up to try to make the turning towards the market before the queen's soldiers got there. They got to the turning first but as they turned into the street, they came across a cart blocking their way and surrounding the cart were three more soldiers. They reined in quickly and went to turn their mounts back the way they had come but the four mounted outriders had closed the gap and were now blocking the entrance.

"Who are you?" one of the mounted soldiers demanded.

"I am Shaeglin," the guide replied. "And we are running late if we are to make camp before nightfall."

"I know who you are," said the soldier. "There are but half a dozen men crazy enough to guide people through the great forest, and you are all well known. I was enquiring after your comrades here."

As he was talking, he dismounted and passed his reins to the soldier next to him, he walked across to Anna, never taking his eyes off her as he did so. On reaching her he took hold of her horse's bridle.

"Dismount," he told her.

Anna shook her head.

"I'm afraid your jurisdiction runs out on the eastern edge of the forest, so if you would kindly remove your cart out of the way." Shaeglin was saying whilst being completely ignored.

"It's her!" The soldier called to the others. He reached up and taking hold of Anna's arm he started to pull her from her saddle.

David sprang into action. He quickly dismounted and reached for his saddle bag. In knowing that he was heading into the forest he had put an axe into one of the saddle bags before they left, he reached for it now and holding it by the axe head he swung the handle end at the back of the soldier's head just as the soldier finished pulling Anna to the ground. The resounding crack as it connected shocked David, but the soldier slumped to the ground and David quickly helped Anna up and put her behind him, between himself and the street wall, as two of the other mounted soldiers dismounted and closed the gap towards them. One of the soldiers peeled off and went to check on his fallen comrade.

"Captain! Captain!" he called as he knelt beside him and shook him by the shoulders. A frown grew on his face as he put a hand to the captain's throat searching for a pulse, and then his head lowered, and he closed his eyes briefly before he once again rose to his feet. The face that turned towards David was ashen.

"Get her," he told his companion.

The soldier closest to them went to step past David to get to Anna, as he did so David closed the gap and hit him hard with his left fist, sending the outrider sprawling off balance. In doing so he opened any possible guard to his left-hand side and the second soldier stepped in and hit him with a closed fist around the hilt of his sword. David dropped to his knees as unconsciousness enveloped him.

The outriders tied up both Anna and David. They dropped Anna at the front of the cart in amongst their supplies that were piled there and tied the end of the rope to a metal loop attached to the side. David, they threw onto the back of the cart. As the soldiers were dealing with the two of them Shaeglin melted back into the crowd of stall holders and shoppers that had started to build up in front of the cart as people craned their necks to see what was going on. Instead of merely looking for a chance to escape, he started to work his way through the crowd, picking out the biggest looking men and the toughest looking women, talking in their ears, encouraging them to react.

"This isn't right," he said to one. "These are not our soldiers, they are outriders from the east, they don't have any power on our streets."

The big man nodded and took a few steps forward, moving closer through the crowd.

Shaeglin picked out a hard looking woman who already looked irate and was frowning at the soldiers as if she were just about to wade in anyway.

"These young people are our people, they deliver wood and bread through our streets," he said to her. "Are we going to just stand aside and let foreign soldiers attack them in our own town? That could be your son or daughter dumped on that cart. If we let them do this, what next?"

He worked his way through the crowd, and gradually a low rumble started, like distant thunder, gradually building up, rolling in. The six soldiers that were left moved forward to line the front of the cart and prepared themselves for a riot. Shaeglin and an accomplice he had picked from the crowd moved over to the side by the wall and as the wings of the mob moved in on the edges of the soldiers, they slipped through along the wall towards the back of the cart.

David came too once, very briefly, as he was carried down some stairs. It was dark, he could smell stale beer, and then he was lowered to the floor and unconsciousness took him again.

# 4

Light returned slowly. Sharp pinpricks of light mixed with blurred images. Daylight was coming subtly through the windows. The smell of ale was gone, but David was struggling to focus on anything. As things started to become clearer and he could make sense of the shapes and items around him, they started to become familiar, familiar but all wrong. He wasn't meant to be here, he had no purpose here, and panic was setting in. His head hurt, and the dizziness was making him feel nauseous. What he had thought was a ringing in his ears caused by the blow to his head, turned out to be the phone ringing, the phone in his cottage in the woods.

Holding his head in one hand he picked up the receiver.

"Hello?"

"Hello? David? Where the hell have you been?"

It was Jeannie's voice on the other end.

"Hello Jeannie, sorry I've been…elsewhere."

"I've been phoning all day, off and on, I wanted to make sure you got back alright from the pub last night, after that bit of trouble."

"Last night? I've been gone for months."

There was a pause from the other end of the line.

"Months? David, what are you talking about? Are you ok? You sound pretty rough."

"I've been unconscious, I'm feeling a bit sick, but I'm alright."

"Unconscious? What happened, did you get into a fight?"

"Yes. No. Not here, somewhere else. Jeannie, I think I killed a man. I've got to get back there! Anna's in danger."

"Who? David, you're not making any sense, you sound delirious. I'm going to go and get Tim and we'll come straight over.  Stay there, alright?  It's going to be dark soon."

Jeannie hung up and David slumped back on the sofa. None of this was making any sense at all.  He couldn't possibly have dreamt all that, all that otherworld, all those months spent with Anna.  He looked around his cottage, it seemed emptier than he remembered.  It had never bothered him, living out here on his own, he had enjoyed the peace and quiet.  Now it felt like it haunted him, like it had stolen something from him, like something was missing.

He was still sat there staring into nothing when Jeannie and Tim pulled up outside his cottage and walked up the steps to knock on the door.  He got up and wobbling a little, he let them both in.

Jeannie had been listening to her friend with growing concern.  David had sat back down on the couch and Jeannie and Tim had joined him in the lounge while he tried to explain what had happened.  At one point, when he spoke of Anna and the soldiers, he got up and started to pace the room, clearly agitated, and repeating over and over that he had to get back there.  Jeannie and Tim had been exchanging glances at each other and eventually Jeannie had said that she would put the kettle on and make some drinks, and Tim had followed her out there to help.

"He needs to go to a hospital," said Jeannie.  "That or a shrink."

"A hospital maybe.  It's certainly a strange tale," said Tim as he passed her the milk.

"A strange tale?  Tim, he believes this happened!" she said, lowering her voice.

"Mm, I've never seen concussion like this before, but I'm no expert."

"He said he got knocked out in that otherworld, not this one!"

"Yes, um, you know him much better than me, has he ever been known to do drugs?"

"Tim! No, nothing like that."

"Sorry, I'm just trying to tick things off the list of possibilities. It's like he's hallucinating. He knows the forest well. He couldn't have picked a wrong mushroom?"

Jeannie chuckled.

"I'm glad you're here to keep the humor in things. No, he knows every inch of this place, his grandmother was a good teacher." Jeannie grew serious again. "It's that that worries me. He's been on his own out here for so long, you hear of people, you know, spending too long in their own company."

"You think I'm going mad."

They both turned to find David standing in the doorway to the kitchen.

"No David, I don't think you're going mad. I think you've had one hell of a knock on the head, and I think you need to go to hospital and get it checked out."

David shook his head.

"What I told you happened, happened. I'm sure of it. It doesn't make any sense to me either, but it was too real not to be."

"The trip to the hospital isn't about that David," said Tim sympathetically. "We can try to get to grips with that later, but any serious head injury should be checked out, you know that. The fact is you've been concussed, and if there is any internal bleeding or anything…it really should be looked at."

David nodded slowly.

"I guess you're right, but I'm coming home when we're done," he said, turning back into the lounge.

"Thank you," Jeannie whispered to Tim.

Nothing had shown up at the hospital. They told him to go home and rest, so Jeannie and Tim took him back to his cottage. They had wanted to stay to keep an eye on him, but David told them he would rest better without Jeannie fussing over him and so they eventually left, both telling him to ring them if he started to feel ill at all. He told them he would, he thanked them both, and assured them he would do what the hospital told him to do, and rest, but rest was the last thing on his mind. The first thing on his mind was Anna.

He laid back on the sofa, turned on the music, put on the headphones, closed his eyes, and crossed his fingers that it worked a second time.

He awoke in the dark, he wasn't sure where. He reached up to his head and couldn't feel any headphones, but he could have knocked them off whilst asleep. He felt below him and could feel wooden boxes, not a soft sofa. The smell of stale beer had returned, and David realized he must be back in the cellar of the pub where somebody had carried him and set him down previously. If it was the same tavern in which he had worked, then Azron would be here and David could get information, and help.

As his eyes adjusted to the dimness of the cellar, he looked around him. Over towards the far end of the room he could see two flights of stairs. One went up to a hatch which he assumed opened onto the street, the other went up to a door. As he had no idea from here whether it was day or night, the street hatch didn't seem like a good idea. If he was in the Bear then he knew the cellar door came out between the kitchen and the bar, away from the public, and that would be his best chance to find out if the coast was clear or if the soldiers were still about. He made his way to the top of the stairs and opened the door a crack, through the gap he could see the back of Azron as he served his customers at the bar. As the bar looked quite busy David guessed that it must be evening, which would help him if he had to move quickly.

"Psst, Azron!" he called in a low whisper.

The bartender turned halfway around but glanced into the kitchen before turning back to the bar to continue serving his customers.

"Psst, Azron, down here!" David repeated.

This time the big man turned and looked around at a lower level and caught sight of David crouching through the crack in the door.

"Excuse me one moment," he said to the customer. "I have to pop down to the cellar."

David retreated down the stairs when he saw Azron had spotted him. He waited for the barman to make his way through the door and down the stairs towards him. David wasn't sure what reception he would get, whether Azron would be happy to see him turn up here again, he had helped them once, but David was aware he was putting the landlord at risk. He needn't have worried, Azron got to the bottom of the stairs, grinned at David and hugged him, almost squeezing the breath from him.

"David!" Azron exclaimed. "I am so happy to see you! We thought maybe the queen's soldiers had you too!"

"No," replied David. "But they still have Anna then?"

The tavern owner nodded sadly.

"Shaeglin stirred up a swarm. He got the crowd at the marketplace infuriated at the soldiers, and when the crowd moved in, he and his accomplice lifted you from the cart the soldiers had dumped you on and brought you back here, but when they went back for Anna the cart was heavily guarded again. The crowd's riot hadn't lasted very long against trained soldiers. The queen's soldiers broke the ribs and nose of one man in the first attack and ran another through with a sword, and the crowd quickly decided they didn't really want any more of it. At that point the soldiers must have noticed you were gone and tightened up the security around their main prize. Shaeglin stood no chance of getting her free at that point, and shortly after the soldiers and the cart moved on. When he came back here to check on you, you were gone. How did you get back in here again?" Azron asked, looking around and glancing at the street hatch, locked from the inside. "And where the hell have you been for the last month?"

"Month?" David blurted out. "I...I'm not quite sure what happened, I took a hefty whack on the head from that soldier, it's all been very vague."

"Well," said Azron, clapping him on the shoulder. "You are back, and now you need to leave."

David raised his eyebrows.

"You killed a queen's captain, David. After the first group of soldiers left with Anna, a couple of weeks ago another bunch turned up. They will be looking for you, don't let them catch you. Our soldiers are wise to them being here now and are keeping them on the move, but they keep floating back, they're unlikely to give up. I need to get back to my customers before any of my staff come looking for me and spot you down here. I will send a runner to go and get Shaeglin, unlock that street hatch while I'm gone, and I will tell him to stop alongside with a spare horse. And David?"

"Yes?"

"Good luck. You are going to need it."

David sat at the campfire with Shaeglin, they had ridden all through that night and the following day. Eventually they pulled off the road and made camp, both the horses and their riders needed to rest. They made it out of town without any issues this time and had entered the forest just as the first daylight was showing on the horizon. As light started to filter through the trees David was amazed by the great woodland around them. Huge ancient trees as far as the eye could see in every direction, moss covered rocks and branches, and a feeling of wildness that he had never experienced before. Shaeglin told him that for now at least they needed to stick to the road, there were other tracks that led off into the trees, but they weren't really fit for travel. As they rode, David caught sight of these tracks, they were not very wide and low branches in places would make it hard to ride at any speed. He could see why the guide wasn't keen to head off the main road.

During their ride David had also caught a glimpse once or twice of another rider through the trees, an older looking man on a grey horse, following a vague route parallel to theirs, and somehow keeping pace, appearing momentarily through the day. David had mentioned it to Shaeglin who had shrugged and told him not to worry, the man was nothing to do with the queen. David hadn't had a chance to question him further as their energies and concentration were needed for the journey ahead. As they sat around the fire discussing their route, David decided he would like to know who else was keeping them company.

"The old man I saw in the distance through the trees, who was he? David asked. "Is he real, or a ghost?"

"He is known as the watcher," replied the guide. "He is real enough, though nobody knows exactly who he is or where he's from."

"But you said he is safe?"

"I said we need not worry," said Shaeglin. "He is known as a guardian."

"Guardian of what?"

"Of the forest. It's said he keeps watch of the forest and the people in it. Those who live in it, those who travel through. He is not always safe, he has been known to even out the numbers if humble travelers are attacked on their travels, protecting them, more than efficiently. He has become a living legend, there is quite a mystery surrounding him. There has been reports of a watcher in these forests for many a year, some claim it has always been the same man, but that is strictly impossible. As for us, we are not here to harm the forest, or anyone within, so we have no cause to fear him."

David glanced behind him at the dark shadows surrounding the light from the campfire, imagining the old man keeping watch over their camp. He wasn't sure if it felt like a comfort or not.

"You said we head northwest tomorrow, surely we should be heading northeast?" David asked, changing the subject.

"We need to cross the river. It will be best to head towards the hamlet of Oakcastle and use the ford there."

"Is there no crossing on our direct route, without having to take the detour? Surely, we add miles to our journey and a considerable amount of time?"

"There is a bridge to the northeast, but it is not a good idea."

"But is it a more direct route?" asked David.

"It is, but I am here to get you through by the safest route, not necessarily the quickest or the shortest."

"The important thing is to get Anna."

"Anna was taken a month ago, you will not come across her on your route, and it will not solve anything if you do not make it to her at all."

David stared into the fire. If anything happened to Anna, he would take the queen's palace apart stone by stone.

"How many miles does the detour add to our journey?" he asked.

"About a hundred and twenty miles. It will add around three days, maybe a little more if we need to rest the horses."

"Then I guess we'd better turn in for the night. The sooner we are gone in the morning, the sooner we get there."

Shaeglin nodded. "You get some rest. I'll take first watch and I'll wake you when it's your turn to take over."

David left the fire at first light and headed through the trees to their vantage point.  The road had taken them up a steep hill the day before and they had set up camp a little way from the edge, just far enough so the light of their fire couldn't be seen on the top of the hill during the night. From the brow of the hill David could see for miles, tracing the road back through the trees.  He was frowning at the horizon, straining to make out what was causing the small dust cloud that was rising just above the trees and moving slowly along the track.

Light footsteps behind him made him turn, and Shaeglin appeared through the trees and joined him on the brow of the hill.

"You heard them too?" the guide asked.

David shook his head.  "Heard what?"

"Hoofbeats.  A long way off but moving this way."

Shaeglin reached inside his tunic and pulled out a small crude looking telescope made from leather.  He trained it towards a large gap in the forest a little over three miles away and waited.  It wasn't long before the dust cloud entered the gap.

"Soldiers.  My guess would be outriders.  A Dozen possibly.  It's time for us to move, and quickly."

"Can't we hide in the trees here and hope they ride on?"

"Our tracks are fresh on the road.  They will stop where the tracks stop and try to flush us out." Replied the guide as they hurried back to their horses.

"Is Oakcastle safe when we get there?  If we get there?"

"Oakcastle is out of the question now.  We can't outrun those soldiers that far," Shaeglin looked distraught as they mounted and headed back to the road.  "We have no choice. We head for the bridge!"

# 5

They rode hard and soon came to the edge of another clearing in the forest that met gently sloping ground heading downhill towards a large river. The other side of the river the land rose again into another dense patch of forest. There was clearly no other way across the river other than a large ornate bridge spanning the river in the middle of the clearing. Half a mile from the bridge David could make out a figure sat on the bridge, even from this distance the man looked big.

"Who's he?" David called across to Shaeglin.

"He is the guardian of the bridge."

David nodded. "Like the watcher of the forest," he said, nodding back over his shoulder towards the trees.

"No," said the guide seriously. "Nothing like the watcher."

Shaeglin slowed his mount to a trot and gestured to David to do the same.

"David this is deadly serious, I didn't want to bring you here, but we can't hope to outrun those soldiers back there, and if they catch us, we're dead for sure."

"What's the problem?" David asked. The guide had turned as white as a sheet.

"Tell me David, how are you at riddles?"

"I don't know, that's not something that's come up very often. Why?"

"The guardian will ask you a riddle, if you get the answer correct, he will let you pass, if you get it wrong, you will have to fight him." The guide looked uncomfortable. "Nobody has ever defeated the guardian in combat."

"Well, there's always a first time for everything," said David lightly. "Anyway, two heads are better than one, maybe we can work it out together."

"I cannot help you David, I cannot give you any clues."

"Maybe he will ask you instead."

The guide shook his head sadly.

"He will not ask me, I have approached the bridge before, I have answered a riddle."

"What happened?  Did you get it right?"

Shaeglin pulled on his reins and stopped his mount.

"David you are not listening to me!" the guide shouted. "You will have to pay much better attention when he asks you the riddle!  Wake up!  When you get to the bridge the guardian will ask you a question, if you get it right, he will let you cross, if you get it wrong, you die!" he paused to let that sink in.  "It is a fight to the death, and as you can see by the fact he is still here, nobody has ever beaten him. Small armies in fact have never beaten him.  You have no choice but to get the riddle right."

"Then why the hell did you bring me here?!" exclaimed David starting to panic at last.

"Because by now those soldiers will be less than two miles behind us and they will kill us anyway, no questions or riddles asked!"

"So, what happens after he kills me?"

The guide paused for a moment.

"It is called the bridge of bones."

"The bridge of what?!"

David looked down at the bridge they were slowly approaching and realized that what he had assumed were pieces of bleached timber were in fact bleached bones.

"I become building material.  He's a nice chap then this guardian of yours?

"Do not judge him too quickly or too harshly David.  He is a giant, by people's standards, by what is normal in the world.  The people never accepted him, and they cast him out into the forest.  This is the only crossing in several days journeying, so to make a living he set up home here and carried people and horses across the river.  Eventually he grew tired of wading backwards and forwards across the river, and of people's attitude towards him and he decided it would be better to have a bridge. He figured it wasn't fair on the trees to cut them down just so the people didn't have to get their feet wet, so he decided as the bridge was mainly for the people, he would use them to build it instead, quite literally."

"Rather macabre?"

"But he felt no affinity with the people, they had cast him out. He is an intelligent man who was persecuted by unintelligent people, and so he decided the fairest test was to test that very intelligence. Those that thought clearly and got it right could cross the bridge whenever they desired, you only have to get it right once."

"Or get it wrong once, then you help to mend the bridge…" David finished for him.

"Exactly. In his head he is helping to create a better world. Those that don't have the courage to take the test do not have to approach the bridge, although it is a long way around."

"And we don't have a choice."

"No, we don't."

As they got to the end of the bridge the giant was sat cross legged in the middle, tucking into a bowl of something red and sticky.

"Please tell me that what he's eating is not the last fellow to get the riddle wrong?" David muttered to Shaeglin.

Shaeglin chuckled. "Driftberry pie. It's why we stopped briefly yesterday to pick those berries. Just in case. It doesn't hurt to stay friends with these people."

David could hear the giant talking to himself between mouthfuls.

"Mm, mm, I love driftberry pie," said the giant cheerfully tucking into another big mouthful. He glanced up and seeing them for the first time his eyebrows shot up.

"Oooh, company," he said, setting down the bowl and wiping his chin. "A new challenger."

David had been watching the giant's movements. The muscles and sinews in the big man's arms and legs moved swiftly under the skin, like snakes under a blanket. The quick intelligent movements of the man's eyes, he had no doubt at all, he couldn't beat this man in a fight. Even sat crossed legged on the bridge he could see the man was huge. He had to get this right, or he was finished. Sweat was breaking out on his forehead.

"Shaeglin," said the guardian in greeting. "I have not seen you for many a day. You bring a friend with you today."

"I do, guardian, and some driftberries for yourself."

"Most kind. Your friend will still have to pass the test though."

"I understand," replied the guide.

"Does he though? Have you explained the rules?"

"I have."

"And you accept the challenge?" asked the giant, turning to David.

"I do," replied David. "Not much choice really, it's you or a dozen soldiers!"

The guardian looked across at Shaeglin with a smile on his face.

"More challengers?" he asked.

"Very possibly," Shaeglin nodded.

"My bridge is in need of repair," said the guardian cheerfully. "Right," he said clapping his huge hands together. "Your riddle then, are you ready?"

David nodded.

"I can climb, and I can creep.
I can grow in darkness deep.
I can twist, and I can crawl.
I can shorten something tall."

David glanced sideways at Shaeglin who just looked panic stricken.

The guardian saw him look across and turned to Shaeglin.

"You know the rules, you cannot help him, if you cheat you both fight me!"

"I don't think I could help him even if I wanted to guardian."

The giant smiled and turned back to study David. David was suddenly aware of what he had let himself in for. If I don't get this right I'm done for, I'm dead and that's it, I won't ever get to see Anna again, I won't get the chance to save her, I'll be dead and she'll be on her own, left to the queen's devices. He tried to stop panicking and tried to concentrate.

I can climb and I can creep, he thought, is that a mammal? If so, is it one I know? We don't get driftberries in my world, what if it's something I've never heard of? He calmed himself again. Just think of the one's you do know. Squirrels could climb, Koalas, Sloths, Bears, but did they creep? Come back to that, he thought. I can shorten something tall. That put a line through that current list of possibilities. Something tall. Was he right to be thinking of trees? David nodded to himself, they were the tallest thing around here, there were no skyscrapers in this landscape. What could shorten a tree? A beaver could, but could a beaver climb? It could twist under water no doubt, but he wasn't sure of creeping or crawling. Grow in darkness deep. The beavers lodge would be dark.

He looked up and found the guardian studying him. It's funny, thought David, he looks friendly, as if he wants me to get it right.

"Do you have it?" asked the giant.

"A moment longer please?"

The guardian nodded. "Of course."

This has got to be right, thought David, or it's the end. Then, for the first time in a long time he thought of home, of the cottage, of what would become of it if he didn't return. Of all the jobs he had to do around the place and the work inside the surrounding woodland to make sure it all stayed healthy…and then he had it, the answer, or at least he thought he did. It was hard to be sure when your life depended on it.

The guardian was still studying him with a friendly smile.

"I think I have it," said David.

The giant raised his eyebrows. "You think?"

"I'm sure," replied David. "As sure as I can be."

"Go on then."

"Ivy," said David.

The giant grew serious and frowned at David, he rose to his feet and stood up straight, rising to his full height, he was truly huge.

"Ivy?" he repeated. "That's your answer?" he asked sternly.

David ran through it all again, he couldn't think of any other answer, it was going to have to do. He planted his feet a little wider apart, moving one subtly around behind the other, if it was going to come to a fight, he was at least going to be ready.

The guardian studied him a moment longer and then his face split into a grin. He stepped to one side and gestured for them to cross.

"Correct," he said. "What is your name?"

"David."

"You are an intelligent man David, and very brave, you were actually getting ready to fight me if you were wrong, rather than getting ready to run. You may cross. You are welcome to cross at any time."

"Thank you," said David leading his horse across the bridge, closely followed by Shaeglin and his mount.

As they reached the end of the bridge, they could hear hoofbeats up on the hill behind them and the outriders appeared on the skyline. The guardian followed David's concerned look towards the soldiers and then turned back to David and Shaeglin.

"It appears it is going to be a busy day," he said cheerfully. "I would get going if I were you."

They had ridden for four days with no sign of any pursuers. David had turned to look back before leaving the clearing above the bridge and had seen the front group of soldiers hit the bridge at a gallop, they clearly had no intention of stopping to answer a riddle. Whatever their intention may have been it was halted very quickly by the giant, and the soldiers to the rear reined in and regrouped. Whether any of them had passed the test and been allowed to cross, neither David nor Shaeglin planned to hang around to find out. They rode hard and took a couple of rough tracks off the main road, trying as best they could to cover their tracks.

They broke camp that morning and rode through some thick dark woodland that eventually thinned out as it rose uphill to join a ridge. The ridge was a bit rockier than the landscape they had ridden through so far and they dismounted and led their horses. The ridge gave a good view of the landscape around them and once again David was amazed by how beautiful the land was. There were flowers up here on the high ground where the trees thinned out, and now and then David could make out birds of prey wheeling around above the treetops. It had been a beautiful sunny day and David was enjoying the ride, forgetting momentarily the mission they were on, but he was aware of the sun dropping and that they had been riding a long time.

"Have you got somewhere in mind for tonight's camp Shaeglin?" he asked, looking around and seeing nowhere suitable.

"I want to pay an old friend a visit, he will offer us shelter for the night.  It is not much further."

David looked around him again.

"I thought my home was remote.  What sort of person lives all the way out here?"

"One who prefers quiet perhaps," said Shaeglin smiling. "He is an old wise man, some call him a wizard, I wish to ask him for some advice.  We go back a long way, he should be pleased to see us, and he can be trusted."

"Well, shelter for the night will make a welcome change from the campfire, especially if there is a bed on offer."

Shaeglin left the rough track they had been following and headed gradually down the south side of the ridge. Before they got to the thick tree line someway further down the hill, they reached a small stand of trees nestled around a cut in the hillside.  When they got to the trees, Shaeglin turned left back towards the side of the hill, and as David turned to follow, he could see a doorway ahead of the guide leading it would seem, into the hill.  As the guide pulled up outside and slid from his saddle David could see that the door was large, more like a castle gate than a small front door.  Shaeglin approached the door and knocked loudly several times.  The door opened soundlessly, and a cheerful little man greeted them, waving them inside.

"Shaeglin, sir, it's been a long time, do come in, and your friend also," he said looking past the guide to David. "Lowgler has been expecting you, bring your horses, there is stabling on the left."

They entered the building inside the hill and David looked around him.  To the left was a long cave with horse stables set along one side, on the wall on the opposite side were torches set at intervals into the wall.

After they had stabled their horses they crossed back across the entrance hall to a large door, opened once again by the same man.

"Why does the queen want this woman?" asked the old man.

Shaeglin shrugged and they both looked at David. David wasn't sure how much he should tell them, but he couldn't rescue her on his own and there was nobody else to help him.

"Anna told me she used to work in the queen's household as her maid. She worked for her for years, but while the queen grew older, for some reason Anna never seemed to age."

The old man and the guide exchanged glances for the briefest of moments.

"She wasn't sure why she wasn't showing her years," David continued. "But it bothered the queen. The queen believes Anna has a secret she is keeping to herself, so ever since Anna managed to escape, the queen has continued to pursue her."

"I see," said Lowgler.

"I'm glad you do," said David. "None of it makes any sense to me."

He put his plate to one side and stared into the fire, deep in thought. What would happen if he never got there in time, or never found her?

"You look tired," said Lowgler after a moment.

David looked up and nodded. The old man rang a bell and the doorman from earlier entered the room.

"Mancham, could you show David to his room please, our travelers have had a long day."

"Certainly sir," said the man, gesturing to David for him to follow him through a side door.

"Rest for now," Lowgler said to David. "We can discuss things further tomorrow if needs be."


After David left the room, the old man looked back to Shaeglin.

"You are welcome as always Shaeglin, but tell me, why did you decide to bring David to meet me?"

"I thought you would like to meet him."

"Why?"

"Because he is not of this world," replied the guide.

"I had sensed that, but are you sure?"

Shaeglin nodded and repeated what had happened on that day in the marketplace.

"When we lifted him from the cart, we took him to the cellar of the Bear tavern and went back to try to get Anna. It was clear straight away that we weren't going to rescue her, so we returned immediately to tend to David as he was unconscious. When we got there, he was gone, vanished. Then he turns up again a month later back in the cellar. He hadn't come in through the pub and the cellar doors were locked from the inside. The landlord never said anything, but you could see it hadn't gone unnoticed."

"But the cellar of the Bear isn't a portal, surely?" asked Lowgler.

"I haven't heard of any portals, not for many years. I'm not sure how he's getting here and back again, I don't think he knows."

"Is he aware that you know he's not from here?"

Shaeglin shook his head.

"The story is he's from Mizule."

"He certainly has the look of one from the western lands."

"It is where we were meant to be headed before the woman was taken."

Lowgler sat studying Shaeglin.

"I have always admired you Shaeglin, and the way you conduct your business. Escorting people safely through this treacherous land for a tiny fee, rather than the king's ransom they would pay to go by ship. Choosing carefully who you take, making sure that it is only those who deserve safe passage who receive your help and leaving the rogues to fend for themselves."

"Thank you," replied Shaeglin.

"But why this young man?  He has, by his own admission, killed one of the queen's soldiers.  That makes him a wanted man, by her anyway, and you a wanted man by association.  They will know it's you who guides him, you have jeopardized your own safety to help him.  Why?"

"Because I was asked to."

Lowgler's eyebrows rose once again.

"By whom?" he asked.

"The Watcher."

Now he had the old man's full attention.

"The Watcher?  Why would he be interested in helping David?"

Shaeglin shrugged.  "I was approached at my campfire some time ago.  I was told there was a young man arrived in town who would need my help, that the man was with a young woman and the young woman was in danger, that they needed safe passage through the forest."

"You never asked why?"

"The Watcher has saved my life three times in the past. He has never led me the wrong way, I do not question him."

"No, quite right," said Lowgler, deep in thought.

# 6

They all met up again the following morning for breakfast before David and Shaeglin were due to depart and continue their journey. They planned to leave on foot so they could keep to the ridge away from the road. Without the horses it would be easier to travel across the terrain and easier to hide should they need to. Lowgler's servant would take the horses down to the road and meet them at the village of Thorn in a couple of days, keeping an eye out for any soldiers on the road that maybe searching for them. David was keen to be on his way but there were still discussions to be had over breakfast.

"These are restless times indeed," said Lowgler, pouring himself more tea. "The queen grows braver and more powerful as each week passes. It seems, as she is the only royal bloodline left in this world that she thinks the entire world should be under her command, but that was not the agreement that all the different realms signed up to. She only rules the east, that is her only rightful kingdom."

"There is no guarantee that she is the last of the royal bloodlines," said Shaeglin.

"The prophesy?" said Lowgler smiling. "Forever the optimist Shaeglin. It is a nice thought though."

"Prophesy?" asked David.

"There is an age-old prophesy that says one day a man will come with true royal blood, and he will unite the people again and end all the wars. It is spoken about every time this world knows unrest, but it is not a bad thing, it keeps people's spirits up." replied Lowgler.

"On the day when cometh the king," said Shaeglin cheerfully.

"That's a song," said David. "I heard Anna singing it, and…I'd heard the tune before."

"Where?" asked Lowgler.

"Somewhere else," replied David vaguely.

"The song was created out of the prophesy, it is a nice tale, the bards will put music to a nice tale," said Lowgler.

"So where is this king meant to come from?" asked David finishing his cup of tea.

"Somewhere else," replied Shaeglin.

David looked up from his cup and found the other two men studying him.

"What?" he asked. "You…you don't think I'm him, the king I mean?" he turned to Shaeglin. "Is that why you brought me here to meet this old wise man?"

Lowgler was laughing now.

"Don't fret David," he said catching his breath. "You are not the king, now is not the time for the tale to unravel. If the prophesy is to be believed, then there are other things to be considered that are not included in the song. But for now, I believe breakfast is finished, and I know that you have been itching to get on your way. My servant Mancham has put some food together for you for your travel, and I wish you well on your quest, I do hope you are successful David."

"Thank you," replied David. "And thank you for your hospitality. It's been good to sleep on a bed for a night and have a belly full of food."

David shook hands with Lowgler and left the room to sort out his pack and wait for Shaeglin.

"So, was that it?" asked Lowgler after David had left. "Did you think he was the king in the prophesy?"

"It is true, I did wonder if he was the one."

The old man shook his head.

"The game has not yet started, there are many moves yet to take place, I think. But it is possible that the pieces are on the board. Take care Shaeglin, of yourself and young David."

"I will old friend. I will see you again soon."

"Make sure you do," said Lowgler smiling. He waved his friend goodbye.

After David and Shaeglin had left, the old man sat for a while with his thoughts. Eventually he got up and moved over to his desk. There were letters to write, there were things to do.

David and Shaeglin walked all day, they kept to the high ridge and saw nobody else. The land was so peaceful and untarnished, it was like something out of a dream. To their left the land dropped away a little before rising further still into a mountain range to the north. Shaeglin told David that beyond the mountain range the land flattened out again onto open plains and smaller woods and hills. There were no real towns to the north, the people there were nomads, moving constantly with their cattle and families to wherever the best grazing was at the time. Although there would occasionally be skirmishes between the tribes it was generally a peaceful land, but a hard one, it was cold up there, and the tribes were not wealthy.

To their right the great forest swept down and away as far as the eye could see. David wondered how far they had come from Selaster, and then found it strange that he almost considered that as home, after all the time he had spent there. It was where he had lived and worked, where he had met Anna. Thinking of her again, he wondered if he did manage to find her and rescue her, where they would live. Would they return to Selaster or would they maybe find a place up here in the quiet wilderness, away from the towns.

For the first time in several days his spirits were high, he could envisage finding Anna and getting her to safety, he could see a day when they would be together again.

"You seem cheerful today, David," said Shaeglin.

"It's hard not to be, surrounded by this scenery. This really is a beautiful land. I was just thinking, maybe I will ask Anna if she would rather live up here than down in the town."

"Ah," said Shaeglin. "My optimism must be rubbing off on you. Let's hope it continues, we have a long couple of days walking ahead of us."


They made camp that night on the northern side of the ridge in a small clearing between a thick line of trees. They shared stories and jokes and enjoyed some of the food that Lowgler had given them, along with a flask of wine Shaeglin had found tucked into his pack. They took turns at keeping watch, even high up on the ridge as they were, they weren't taking any chances.

As daybreak arrived, they had breakfast and kicked out the last of the fire, put on their packs, lighter now after the food and wine consumed, and set off on their way. Bit by bit they started to descend as the ridge slowly lowered back towards the forest. The trees became denser again, and they had to navigate past debris in places as the path they were on was seldom trodden.

It was Shaeglin's turn to be in high spirits today as they walked along through the trees. He was telling David tales of his various travels through the forest and the characters he had met along the way. After a while they stepped out of the trees into a clearing in the forest. It was a gently sloping piece of land, a few acres of grassland with half a dozen large boulders dotted about amongst the tall grass. Sheaglin was busy telling David about the last time he had travelled the ridge and dropped in on Lowgler, when suddenly the guide stopped dead in his tracks and put an arm out in front of David to stop him also. When David looked across at the guide, Shaeglin had a finger over his lips to signal David to stay quiet. The guide had gone very pale, and sweat was breaking out on his forehead. He signaled to David for them to slowly retrace their steps and they walked backwards towards the cover of the trees.

"What's wrong?" asked David.

Shaeglin shook his head, looking extremely worried.

"Do you have bears where you come from David?" he whispered.

"Not in my country," David whispered back. "Not anymore."

"I can't believe I've been so stupid! Why wasn't I paying attention? I've been through this way enough times to spot a change in the landscape, I've acted like a complete novice!"

David looked around him. They had just stepped back passed the last boulder, but they were still some way from the cover of the trees. David was searching around the clearing for any signs of an elusive bear as he continued to keep in step with Shaeglin. He was beginning to think the guide was having him on when he spotted movement from the nearest boulder. He looked around the boulder trying to see what was hidden behind it when another movement made him draw in a breath. What had moved was the boulder itself. What he had thought was a split in the rock turned out to be the gap between a paw and the creatures head. The gap opened as the paw moved outwards allowing a large muzzle to raise itself and sniff the air. The nose clearly detected a scent, and then the eyes opened. Deep amber, all animal, and fixed directly on David. The stare was almost enough to freeze the blood in David's veins. The beast rose up and bellowed and suddenly the landscape shifted. Instead of a peaceful glade containing grass and boulders there was a small clearing with half a dozen huge ferocious bears.

"Rock bears! Run!" shouted Shaeglin. "Into the woods!"

Shaeglin was several paces ahead of David as he turned and sprinted in the direction of the trees. David could feel the ground shaking beneath him and knew without turning that the creatures were in hot pursuit. As he neared the edge of the trees David could hear the breath of the nearest bear and knew that he wasn't going to make it to safety. He saw Shaeglin head off to his right where there appeared to be a huge thicket of brambles and so he followed in the same direction. As Shaeglin approached the brambles, in one movement he slid his legs out in front of himself and dropped to the ground, disappearing backwards on his belly into a ground level gap in the briars, a smeuse leading under the brambles. David was preparing himself to copy the guides movements when he was shoved forwards from behind and fell, rolling in a tangle of limbs. He had stopped about thirty feet from the gap and knew he couldn't cover that distance in time. The bear had stopped and was pawing the ground, recovering its breath from the chase. David guessed the bear also knew that the distance to safety was too great as it seemed in no hurry to finish off its prey. He slowly rose to his feet and keeping one eye on the bear he searched around for a makeshift weapon, finding a solid branch just off to his left, he made a sudden dash for the thicket. The quickness of movement caused the bear to move in for an attack and David swung the branch at the animal's fast approaching face, catching the bear across the nose and opening a gash on its muzzle. The bear roared and snorted at David, splattering him with droplets of blood. David took a few steps back. He had seen polar bears once in a zoo and he figured this chap must be at least the same size. He had never stopped to consider whether smacking a polar bear around the face with a twig would be a good idea because he had never ever dreamed that the opportunity would present itself, but he reckoned now that he was in trouble, big trouble.

The area behind the bear was slowly filling up with other bears, and even if David had a gun on him, he wouldn't have fancied his chances. It happened quickly. Possibly the lead bear decided it didn't want to share its meal with the other bears, or maybe David had just annoyed it. With one swipe of its paw, it knocked the branch from David's hand and then the next paw caught David across the chest just below his right shoulder. The blow sent him flying backwards and he landed on his back a few feet from the thicket with his feet facing the brambles and the top of his head facing the bear. His chest was a blazing fire of pain and his breath had been knocked out of him. Above him, he could see the bear slowly approaching and there was nothing he could do about it. He didn't even have the breath in his lungs to attempt to move. As he closed his eyes and waited for the end, he could feel himself being dragged across the forest floor. A shadow fell over him and he knew these were his last few moments.

When the attack didn't come, realization came instead. He was being dragged by his feet, not by his top half, so he must therefore be being dragged towards the thicket and not back towards the bears. He dared to open his eyes and above him all he could see was brambles just above his face, until eventually the roof of briars rose further to create a natural shelter and he stopped being dragged. Appearing by the side of him, kneeling and bending over him, was Shaeglin.

"We are safe in here, the bears won't bother to fight their way through this lot, there will be easier takings elsewhere, they will get bored soon enough," said the guide. "David, I thought you were a dead man."

"So did I," said David weakly. "Thank you, my friend."

The guide nodded.

"You were fortunate he knocked you close enough. I have to say, I have never heard of anyone daring to hit one of those things in the face before! You know, sometimes I question your sanity."

The guide was trying to make light of the situation but as he started to look at the extent of the wound on David's chest, he started to frown."

"David! David you are…fading. Oh, my word, you are disappearing! Listen, if you can hear me, if you come back, meet me at Thorn, I will wait for you there. David, can you hear me?"

His voice grew faint until David could no longer hear what he was saying. David's sight blurred and weakened as if he were passing out, he wondered if he was dying after all, and then Shaeglin's voice was replaced by another.

"David! Can you hear me? Tim, I think he's coming around. David?"

"The ambulance is on its way," replied another voice.

"Where has all this blood come from? He wasn't like this when we got here. Tim, what's going on?"

David's sight drifted back into focus. Above him was the face of a woman, tearful, concerned, Jeannie's face. He was back in his cottage, back on his sofa, and in a lot of pain.


David looked out of the car window at the forest passing by. The valleys and the Scots pines, the heather and the bracken, the ponies and the cattle. He would miss the forest, he was sure of that, it had been there his entire life, whenever he needed it, but when he entered that otherworld again, he vowed never to return here. He would find a way to stay there by whatever means possible, until he found Anna, or died trying. Lord knew how much time had passed again whilst he was at the hospital.

He shifted slightly in his seat looking for a more comfortable position. The wound didn't hurt so bad now that it had been stitched up, and it hadn't been nearly as bad as they thought it was. Ten stitches, it would be enough to leave a scar.

"Are you sure you want to go back to the cottage David? You could stay at mine, or even at Tim's if you wanted to?" asked Jeannie.

Tim turned in the front passenger seat and gave a small nod to David.

"No, the cottage will be fine Jeannie," replied David. "Thanks anyway, but I'm hardly an invalid and I'd rather be at mine."

"So that you can go back to your otherworld again?"

David leaned in slightly so he could see Jeannie's eyes in the rearview mirror. She didn't look angry, so he smiled back.

"You believe me now then?"

"I have to I suppose, one way or another. The doctor spoke to me at the hospital, he asked me what zoo you worked at, and what attacked you, I said probably a chainsaw and he just frowned, he said the wound looked like a scratch from a large animal, I just shrugged and said I didn't know. So, what did attack you?"

"A bear," David replied.

Tim was looking out of the passenger window. David was sure he was laughing silently.

"A bear?!" exclaimed Jeannie. "What the hell were you doing that close to a bear?!"

"Trying to get less close to a bear," said David.

Tim cleared his throat and turned again to look at David.

"What sort of a bear was it, David, was it a big bear?"

"Think along the lines of a polar bear," said David. "A hungry one."

Tim raised his eyebrows and the humor disappeared from his face.

"Seriously? That's not fun."

"It wasn't particularly enjoyable, no." said David. He didn't add that he was laying on the ground with his eyes closed waiting for it to kill him. They didn't need to know that.

"So, are there any more dangerous animals in this otherworld of yours David?" asked Jeannie.

"Not that I'm aware of, the bears came as a bit of a shock. It had been quite pleasant up until then, well, apart from the soldiers."

"Soldiers?" asked Tim.

David nodded. During the rest of the journey home, he told them what had happened since he first arrived there. When he got to the part about killing the captain, Jeannie and Tim looked a bit uncomfortable until he explained exactly what had happened and that it was an accident. He told them about meeting Anna, about getting to know her, and about their time together. He told them about losing Anna, and then he went quiet and stared out the window again, lost in his thoughts.

Tim watched him for a few moments and then glanced across to Jeannie in the driving seat before facing front again and looking out of the window.

"Do you know? I don't think I've ever really spent enough time in this forest. I don't think I've ever really appreciated it," he said cheerfully. Jeannie glanced across at him and just continued driving. "I've often thought it would be nice to stay in a remote cottage out here and soak it all in a bit more," he continued. "I could close the shop for a few days and bunk off, have some fresh air and recuperation. What do you reckon Jeannie?"

"I'd been thinking the same thing," she replied. "I haven't had a holiday or a sick day for ages, I'm sure I could swing a few days off."

David turned away from the window again and back into the car.

"You don't have to babysit me," he said. "I'll be fine. I don't know how long I'll be gone for, and you both have your own lives to live. You don't have to worry."

Tim turned in his seat again.

"You were maybe lucky the last time, you know? You were out of it when we first entered the cottage, but you weren't bleeding at that point. Jeannie kept an eye on you while I went and put the kettle on, and then suddenly…” Tim shook his head. “If we hadn’t been there at that precise moment, you could have bled to death.  What happens if you fall foul of another one of those bears, or some of those soldiers get hold of you?  It maybe won’t hurt to have somebody here just in case.  Unless you want us to join you there?  If you put the music on and we all join hands or something?  I mean, I’ve never wielded a sword or fired an arrow properly, but I’m sure I could learn, if you want some extra help?”

David grinned at him.

“I think I’m probably enough of a liability in that world. There are people there who will help me who know the land well.  I think while I’m looking after me, I’d rather not have a couple more like me to worry about.  If that makes sense?”

“Understood,” said Tim.

“If you want to stay in the cottage for a couple of days you are welcome to, but I don’t want to be disturbed while I’m gone, I’ll come back in my own time.  That’s if I can get back there in the first place, there’s never any guarantee.”

They had something to eat back at David’s cottage and talked things through.  Then David settled back on the sofa with the music drifting through his headphones while the other two busied themselves in the kitchen.  It was agreed David would try to re-enter the otherworld and so long as he didn’t appear seriously injured at any point the others would leave him to it.  If at any stage they had to get back to their jobs, if he was gone a long time, then they were to leave him, not wake him, as he thought it likely this would be his last chance of finding Anna alive.

# 7

When David came to, he was on a track in the woods, it was dawn, and there was a light drizzle.  He wasn't sure where in the forest he was but a little way ahead of him he could just make out a road.  The forest was quiet save for the bird song and the light breeze through the treetops.  David headed for the road and turned right, hoping that was the way that would lead him to the village of Thorn.  He hoped he hadn't been gone so long that Shaeglin had given up on him, he would need the guide's help to complete his mission.

After half a mile he came to a crossroads, to his relief the crossroads had a signpost.  The sign pointing left merely said "North", to the right it read "The Swathes" twenty miles, and the sign ahead "Thorn" five miles.  He had the whole day ahead of him, he thought he should be able to cover that distance by lunchtime.

He set off at a comfortable pace, keeping close to the edge of the road so he could head for cover quickly if he needed to.  He wondered what Thorn would be like in comparison to Selaster, the only town he had seen so far in this world.  He had to find Shaeglin when he got there but he would have to be careful not to draw attention to himself.  Maybe when he got near it would be better to wait and approach the town under cover of darkness.

He continued along the road as it gently meandered through the forest.  He had gone about a mile and a half from the crossroads when he became aware that he could hear horses.  The trees muffled and distorted the sound somewhat so at first, he wasn't sure what direction they were coming from until they turned the corner behind him.  David left the road quickly, but not before one of the riders spotted him and called out.  David didn't wait to find out who they were and instead headed off through the trees like a startled deer.  Bounding over small brooks, boulders and bracken, ducking under low branches, he picked a route he knew the horses couldn't follow, hoping it would be enough.

It wasn't.  One of the riders dismounted as soon as their way was blocked and gave chase.  The other zigzagged through the trees on whichever route he was able to take his horse.  Still not fully recovered from the bear attack, David tired before his pursuer, and as he felt his stride start to shorten, he also caught sight of the rider a little way off to his right.  He could hear the man on foot crashing through the forest behind him and knew he couldn't outrun them.  It was time to make a stand.  As he approached a large oak tree, he scouted the ground for something he could use as a weapon, finding a fallen branch small enough to swing but hefty enough to carry a threat, he turned to face his attacker.  The man was so close to David that as he came crashing past the last tree concentrating on where he was putting his feet, he didn't have time to put the brakes on and draw his sword.  As he glanced up to check how far his quarry now was ahead of him, he came face to face with a swinging lump of wood.  David dropped the branch and knelt to check the man was out cold, noticing the uniform and realizing they were two more of the queen's men.  As he stood up, he heard the rider approaching at speed.  He just had time to grab the stricken soldier's sword and face the new attack.  The rider came in with such a forceful blow that David's hurried grip on the sword was quickly lost, as he tried to raise it to defend himself the sword was sent flying and David was knocked off his feet onto his back.  The rider quickly dismounted and closed the gap, giving David no time to recover.  There was no defense left.  As the soldier raised his sword above his head David waited for the blow that would end it all,

It never came.  In a moment quite surreal, the soldier's features turned from anger to complete surprise as he dropped his sword and slumped to the ground, an arrow through his chest.  David turned abruptly to find the Watcher standing with his feet apart, another arrow already knocked in his bow.

"Where are we heading to?" asked David.

"A camp a little way from here," replied the Watcher.

David had managed to catch the second soldier's horse and had been told by the Watcher to go and find the first rider's horse while he dealt with the soldier.  David wasn't sure what he meant by that and wasn't sure he wanted to know, so he set off to find the other horse.  When he returned there was no sign of either soldier and the Watcher was there with his own horse waiting for him.  David was now riding along behind him, leading the spare horse along a rough track through the thickest part of the forest.

"How did you know I was there?" asked David.

"I didn't, it was pure chance," replied the Watcher.

"Pure luck on my part, I'd have been killed had you not been there."

"That you would."

David continued to ride along behind the Watcher, looking at his back, and thinking.

"And out of all these miles of forest, you just happened to be in the same patch of woods as me?" he asked.

The Watcher glanced back over his shoulder with a slight smile on his face.

"See how lucky you are?"

"I don't buy it," said David.

"Shaeglin said he hoped you'd be making an appearance at some point.  He said he told you to meet him at Thorn and that you would likely be coming from the direction of the crossroads.  You make plenty of noise for a tracker to track."

"Is that what you are?  A tracker?" asked David.

"I track," the Watcher nodded.  "I hunt.  I watch."

David studied the man's back again.  The older man had an air of power about him, and David wondered again who he truly was.

"Shaeglin says you watch the forest," said David.  "That you look after it?"

Silence drifted back.  Whoever he was, he clearly didn't want to discuss it.

After a short time, they dropped down into a natural bowl in the forest, there were beech and oak trees here and the going was a bit easier as there was no thick brush covering the forest floor.  As the land started to rise again, David could see there were some thicker bushes up on the crown of the hill and as they breasted the hill and met the level ground at the top they rode through a gap in the bushes and came across Shaeglin's camp.

"David!" cried Shaeglin, dropping the pan he was cleaning and rising from the log on which he had been seated.  "You made it back safely!"

"Just about," said David.  "My luck hasn't quite deserted me yet."

Shaeglin glanced across at the Watcher.

"He had a run in with a couple of the queen's soldiers."

"They're in the forest?" asked the guide.

The Watcher shook his head.

"Just a couple of scouts," he said.  "The full army is still a few days ride away to the east."

"Army?" asked David.

Shaeglin returned to his log by the campfire and gestured to David to join him.  The Watcher seated himself on another log across the fire from them.  The guide picked up his pan and continued to clean it.

"A lot has happened in a short time whilst you've been away David.  The queen began to make her plans much clearer. She moved a few troops down to two old forts on the edge of the southern lands to repair them and garrison them, the forts are just about on her land but have not been in use for a very long time, not in her lifetime, or her father's either I think. The southern lands counteracted the move by sending some of their own troops to garrison their own fort just inside their own border. After that there were rumors from traders that the queen was amassing an army and the south and west lands took those rumors seriously enough to send in spies, some were found out and killed, but some made it back to confirm that sadly that was happening. That army is now on the move towards the eastern entry to the forest, whether she intends to travel south, or west is unknown. The other governments aren't waiting to find out, they are amassing a joint army of their own on the outskirts of Thorn and intend to intercept her before she enters the forest. They do not want the battle to be brought into the towns on their own lands and there is a flat valley a few miles east of the edge of the forest big enough for two armies to meet, it is the ideal place, if there is such a thing as an ideal place for war."

"So, what is the plan now?" asked David. "If the queen is on the move towards us, does she have Anna with her?"

"We don't know, we can't get close enough to find out. After finding spies in her town the queen has tightened her security."

"Will the south and west's army prevail?"

Shaeglin shrugged. "The queen has a vast army of her own, we can only hope that ours proves stronger."

"If the queen wins, I will have no chance of ever saving Anna," said David.

"It would be a disaster all around," replied the guide.

"In the heat of battle, if Anna is with the queen, even if we win, how is her safety guaranteed?"

Shaeglin looked across the fire towards the Watcher and sat quietly for a moment.

"There is a captain in our army," the guide said. "Captain Ranzard. He is young for a captain, and a little headstrong, but he is a good man, and the men will follow him. He will no doubt be at the frontline of battle and the frontline of the final attack on the queen and her guard, he will make sure he's at the front of it. Your only hope as far as I can see is to talk to him and explain who Anna is, that she is a prisoner, and she is to be spared and ask him to tell his men before the battle to look out for her. And then just hope that in the heat of battle they remember."

"So, where do I find this Captain Ranzard?" asked David, rising to his feet.

Shaeglin gestured for him to sit back down.

"He will be in Thorn," replied Shaeglin. "As will several thousand other soldiers. You cannot go blundering around in there asking for him, nobody knows you, you look like a stranger, and our army is as touchy as the queen's when it comes to strangers at this time. You are likely to be arrested as a spy and locked up somewhere until after the battle. The Watcher will go in at first nightfall, he will find Ranzard and arrange a meeting for later in the night, then you can go and talk to the captain."

David looked across the fire.

"I do not know the Watcher. He tells me nothing of himself. How do I know I can trust him?"

"You don't. But if he wanted you dead, he could have left you to those soldiers back there."

"But who is he?"

Shaeglin looked across the fire, but the Watcher seemed preoccupied with a knife he was sharpening. The guide lowered his voice.

"There is a rumor that claims he is the rightful king of the west, but there has been no royal family there for centuries, so I cannot see how it is so. He would be dead a long time by now."

"So, who was this king?" asked David.

"A long time ago, there was a prince of the west, a proud warrior much loved by his people. It was arranged that he should marry the queen of the east, not this queen of course I'm talking centuries ago. Anyway, the queen was a widow, older than him by a decade or so, and it wasn't her that the prince fell in love with, it was her niece, a princess. Their relationship and the marriage that could have happened could just as easily have united the two lands. You see, the arrangement had originally been made to prevent war. Unfortunately, the queen was jealous, spurned, and angry, she threatened to unleash her entire army on the land unless something was done. The prince's father, the then king of the west, banished them from these lands, never to be seen again. There was nothing else he could do, it threatened all the lands, the civilians, all the peace they had been trying so hard to build. The prince was given a choice, give up the princess, or leave. The prince wouldn't give her up. The way the story is told, I don't think he realized at the time that the princess would be banished as well, I think he intended to come back for her. Neither were seen again. And then, many years later, a stranger was reported travelling through the forest, helping those who needed him, a proud warrior," Shaeglin nodded across the campfire. "With a strange sense of justice."

"And impeccable hearing," said the Watcher. "Campfire stories for your travelers Shaeglin?"

"I have to tell the stories Watcher. You talk too little."

"And you talk too much," said the Watcher rising from his seat by the fire. He looked at David. "I will come back for you later, around midnight. Stay here until I return."

He left them to their fire and led his horse back out through the bushes.

"Whatever the stories, whatever the truth David, I think you should trust him."

"Why?"

"Because he is the one that asked me to help you."

"To find Anna?" asked David.

"No, before that."

"To guide us through the forest?" he asked. "But how did he know?"

The guide shrugged.

"He knew a lot of things. He knew you weren't from Mizule, even though he told me to suggest to you that you were."

David cast his mind back.

"It was you! That's where I knew you from! That day, by the map at the harbor, you were the man that spoke to me then?"

Shaeglin nodded. "Whoever you are, whoever he is, he has been watching you for some time, and if he wanted your quest to fail, he would have ended it a long time ago."

# 8

It was after midnight when the Watcher returned to the camp. The clouds had cleared during the evening and the moon shed a good light across the small clearing. When they heard the approach of hooves Shaeglin picked up his bow and some arrows and stood off to one side with an arrow trained at the gap between the bushes, but when he saw who it was, he relaxed and returned to the fire. The Watcher led his horse to where the other mounts were tethered and approached the campfire, signaling David to stay seated as he started to rise from his seat.

"Change of plan," said the Watcher. "We will go just before first light."

"Why the wait?" asked David.

"They expect the battle to be the day after tomorrow, so tonight, the soldiers have been drinking, telling tales of past glories, and building up one another's courage. Whatever you told them tonight, I doubt they would remember tomorrow. The town was starting to quieten as I left. The soldiers will be at their training grounds first thing in the morning, there will be sore heads, but most will be sober, or sober enough, we meet Captain Ranzard and his men at their grounds at first light. Have your speech prepared."

"And how about you?"

"What about me?" asked the Watcher.

"Will you be there to lend support, or are you just there as a guide to show me to their grounds?"

The Watcher glanced across to Shaeglin, but Shaeglin was busying himself sharpening a knife.

"I'm sorry," replied the Watcher. "I don't understand what…"

"You understand more than me!" said David. "By all accounts you understand quite a lot! I, on the other hand, know nothing. How I got here, why I am here, where here even is! You have been tracking me, it would seem, almost from day one. Would it hurt your aloofness so much to give me some answers?"

"What have you been telling him Shaeglin?" the Watcher asked.

"Nothing more than what you heard before you left. Rumors, that is all they are, stories I hear from other travelers, I have no more information than that."

"Ah! This land thrives on myths and legends," said the Watcher throwing more wood on the fire. "And prophesies."

"Is none of it real then? asked David.

"Real? Define real. Define imagination. Does everything have to be so black and white? Your world is so advanced David, and yet it has fallen so far behind."

"What do you mean?"

"Look around this glade, what do you see?"

David was not sure what the old man was getting at, but he looked around the clearing anyway.

"You, me, Shaeglin, the horses?" David shrugged.

"Anything else?"

"Trees?"

The Watcher chuckled.

"Now relax. Sit back and breathe. Forget about all the things you were trying to accomplish, forget about your life in your world, forget about your life in this one, clear your mind and just be. For one moment, however brief, just live in the moment, here and now and nowhere else. Open your mind."

While the Watcher had been talking, David had noticed the light subtly changing. He had done as he was asked and cleared his mind of all the worries and challenges, of all the thoughts and questions, and relaxed. He was aware of his breathing, of the light breeze tugging gently at the treetops, and the crackle of the fire. And then gradually, he was aware of more.  At first it was movement at the edge of the clearing, seen out of the corner of his eye, assumed to be one of the bushes moving in the breeze, and then came more.  A face in the trunk of a tree.  No, not in the trunk, between the trunk and a bough, attached to a torso and limbs, wiry, woody, as if growing out of the tree, until it moved and scampered along the branch before turning to look at David once again.  Smaller things with wings flitting from tree to tree, then a few of them by the fire, dancing, and two on the log opposite seemingly talking to the Watcher.  Then something much larger towards the back at the edge of the trees, in the shadows.  Antlers, tall, the biggest stag David had ever seen.  But not a stag.  Below the antlers, a man, his head and torso barely visible in the dappled moonlight.  Quiet power, watching, studying.  David's nerves were on edge.  He looked across the fire to the Watcher.

"What are all these things?"

The question evaporated everything.  Back to a clearing, moonlight, trees, and flickering shadows.

There was something sad in the Watcher's smile.

"And still man must question, must know, and with the questions come answers, and with the answers, the magic is lost.  They are the owners of the forest David, of all the land, if you can say any of it has an owner," he studied David.  "Did you think I was looking after it for us?  For humans?  Humans will look after their own affairs.  There are few in this world now who know these things even exist, even fewer in yours.  They will tell you these woods are haunted, but they cannot tell you what by.  In your world they have been pushed to the far corners, to the outer edges, and even then, man must stamp his foot in the mud just to leave a mark and show he's been there," he put another log on the fire.  "Myths, legends, memories, truth, it all gets mixed up in the end."

"So, is it you?  Are you him?"

"Who?"

"The prince in the tale. Banished from these lands because of his love for a princess?"

"What if I were? What difference would it make?"

"It would be a piece of the puzzle," said David. "It might help explain why you spend your time wandering alone through this forest. Is she here too, in these woods?"

The Watcher stared across the fire at David, it was as if his eyes burned hotter than the flames. David couldn't meet his gaze.

"No," the Watcher quietly replied. "She's dead isn't she, they're all dead. Centuries have gone by, generation after generation, you talk of a time long since passed."

"Why trouble yourself with me then? Why look out for me? Why help me?"

"It's what I do isn't it? Listen to the stories. I help travelers. It's obvious you aren't from here, if you are from somewhere else and you are here then you have traveled, haven't you? You are a traveler who needs my help."

"That's somewhat vague."

The Watcher smiled.

"Look, all that matters for now is that you get Anna back safely, right? How is having all these answers going to help you do that? The queen has Anna, the queen has an army, we have an army, and somewhere in all the melee you need to find Anna. Those are the facts you need, anything else is clutter, and you will need your mind as clear as possible to enable you to act quickly."

"That makes sense I suppose, but…"

"Your only tie in this world is Anna. Why bind yourself to other troubles which are not yours?"

David stared into the flames. What the old man was saying was true, Anna was all that mattered, the politics and battles in this world were not his business and the more he got involved in life in this world, the more he would have to deal with. But that didn't help him to answer what he was doing here in the first place.  When he looked up from the fire to speak some more, the Watcher had settled back on the ground and was snoring.  David looked across to Shaeglin who was spreading his own blanket out.

"Better get some sleep David," said the guide.  "I don't think any of this is going to get any easier."

A few hours later they kicked out the fire and broke camp.  Leading their horses down from the hill and along a track that only the Watcher could see in the darkness.  The other two followed him one by one, nobody spoke in the early morning silence of the forest.  The sun was yet to rise, and the birds had not begun their early morning melody.  A voice could travel far in the stillness, much further than they could see.

They continued to wind their way through the forest, keeping well away from the road, until eventually they reached the edge of the trees and stepped out into a small field that sloped down towards the back of a large village.  Once out of the darkness of the forest David could see that dawn was slowly approaching.  The Watcher led them around the back of the houses and stores, staying away from the main street until they got to the far end of the village.  Here there was a large flat area, possibly used as a cattle market at certain times of the year, but right now it was beginning to fill with soldiers and the sound of weapons clashing.  The Watcher took them off to the left towards a marked-out area under some large pines that would afford some shade when the sun was high.  The three men found a spot under one of the pines and waited for day to break.

They waited there a while watching the various troops arriving and heading to their own training grounds.  The area in front of the pine trees slowly filled up as the men paired off and started their warm-ups with swords and spears.  Nobody paid much attention to the few men sat in the shade under the trees.

After a short time three men arrived at the training ground, the dress and stance of one of the men suggested he was of importance and many of his men briefly stopped what they were doing to acknowledge him. One by one they returned to their training as the three men made their way towards the pines.

The Watcher rose from his seat under the trees and closed the gap between them, nodding to the man in the center before approaching him and shaking his hand. David guessed this must be Captain Ranzard and he stood also, as did Shaeglin, and they stepped out from the trees towards the others. The captain was indeed a young man for his rank, possibly close to David's age, not a huge man but clearly very fit and trained for battle. He had a close-cropped beard and dark hair cut short, he had a sword at his side and a round shield like the rest of his men that was slung over his shoulder across his back, he wore a metal breastplate and thick leather guards on his forearms. He was chatting with the Watcher but kept glancing over the old man's shoulder to the other two men approaching.

"You must be David?" the captain called as David got to within hailing distance.

The Watcher stepped to one side so the two men could meet. David closed the gap and held out his hand that was quickly grasped by the captain. There was little difference in size or age, but even with all his physical work around the forest and his cottage, David still had no doubt that the captain would be trained much harder. The soldier exuded confidence, but it was a friendly greeting that David received.

"It's good to meet you," said Ranzard.

"You too," replied David.

"So, you have come to join our numbers?"

"To join you?" David frowned. "I am not a soldier."

The captain's eyes flicked across to the Watcher, before once again settling on David.

"But the Watcher said you had a woman captured by the queen that you were wanting to rescue?"

"That is true," replied David.

"How do you plan to do that then?"

"I don't know.  I can't be sure if the queen will have Anna with her or whether she is being kept at her castle.  If I go to the castle to try to rescue her, I could be leaving her behind at the battlefield.  In the heat of battle, if she were anywhere near the battlefield or the queen's camp I would fear for her safety.  I was told you would be at the forefront; I was hoping I could ask you and your men to look out for her and safeguard her."

The captain's eyes had narrowed slightly.

"My men and I will be at the forefront," he stated.  "We will be the arrowhead that smashes the queen's center!" as his voice started to rise some of his men stopped their training and moved closer to hear their conversation.  "We will end this threat to our lands once and for all, or we will die trying!  That is our vow, and that is our one concern, I cannot be concerned for one man's wishes if he is not willing to join us.  There will be many dead tomorrow, many of the faces you see on this field this morning you will not see again by tomorrow's end.  They fight for their families; they fight for their loved ones.  And yet, you ask me to risk my men to search for one face among thousands while you wait somewhere in safety, this I cannot do."

David looked hopelessly across at the Watcher.

"Then this has all been for nothing," he looked back at the captain.  "Thank you for your time."

He turned slowly and started to walk away.

"Of course," called the captain.  "If this woman of yours is such a beauty that you were willing to travel so far and go through so much to rescue her, maybe I will offer her to the bravest man on the battlefield tomorrow, maybe that will be just the incentive they need!"

David stopped walking and in one fluid movement he turned and headed back to Ranzard.  All the stress, all the worry, all the disappointment mixed with the man's ridicule proved just too much and he strode straight up to the captain and without saying a word he felled the captain with a big straight right fist.  Some of the soldiers closed around the captain cutting him off from any further threat while a couple of the others took hold of David by his arms.  The anger stirred up in the men was clear to see.

"Wait!" shouted the captain above the murmur of angry voices.

The men parted to reveal the captain laid out on the ground, propped up on his right elbow while his left hand was rubbing the left side of his jaw where David's fist had connected.  David was surprised to find that the man did not look angry.  He was nodding at David with a look of mild amusement on his face.  He slowly rose to his feet and walked up to David.

"If you will excuse the insult?" he said, still lightly rubbing his jaw.  "I had to test you, I had to find out if the rumors were true."

"What rumors?" asked David sternly.

"Your name travels before you.  The man who killed a queen's captain, the man who crossed the bridge of bones, the man who fought a rock bear with a stick and yet still lives!  And then fought more of the queen's soldiers."

"I was bested and saved in three out of four of those," said David lightly.

"Maybe so, but now you can add to your resume, the man who felled Captain Ranzard.  When I hear of a man unwilling to back down, I prefer to find out the truth for myself.  I was concerned that you were about to give up."

"I will find another way," said David.

The captain shook his head.

"There is no other way.  The queen will know her castle is under threat whilst she heads into battle, it will not be empty, it will be heavily guarded, and you will surely get yourself killed. Likewise, you and these two old men will not be able to enter her camp behind the battlefield either, they will be more than prepared for spies and assassins. You will need an army, which you do not have, but we do. And it would be best if you were at the front of that army, to be the first there, which means with us. You need us, and maybe we need you too. A true warrior is worth ten soldiers in battle."

"I am not a warrior," replied David.

"There is only one way to find out, isn't there?" said the captain. He turned to the nearest soldier. "Get this man kitted out, armor, shield, sword. The rest of you, back to training."

# 9

David had grown up reading books on medieval knights, of the rulers, and the battles. Tales of soldiers banding together as one in a shield wall, locking shields, advancing on an enemy. The romanticism of the brave knight in one-to-one combat with an equal as the rest of the battle rages on around them. It was these tales that had made him spend large parts of his childhood playing with bows and arrows and homemade swords and shields with his friends in the woods around his cottage and encouraged him to take up archery lessons and fencing when the chance arose. He had excelled at fencing; he had won trophies. It all meant very little in the reality of battle. Close combat, pressed from all sides with very little room to move, soldiers trying to slash and stab at him from all angles as he and the men around him tried to do the same back. Pushing, always pushing, trying foot by foot to get the enemy moving backwards. Concentrating all the while on staying on his feet, of not going under. Stepping over the bodies of enemies and fallen comrades, and still concentrating on not being the next to join them.

The army had lined up on the battlefield at first light. A huge level plain surrounded by hills. Dawn brought with it a swirling mist and as the mist cleared, they could see the enemy lined up a quarter of a mile away. The queen had amassed a large army, maybe more soldiers than they held in their own ranks. Whichever way the battle went today, it would be hard won.

David lined up in the front ranks of Ranzard's troops, three soldiers to the right of Ranzard himself. The young captain was calling orders to his men, getting them organized, making them concentrate. Captain Ranzard was not the leader of the defending army, that duty fell to the lord of the western lands, Lord Landstral, a tall, imposing man of around fifty. He sat astride a strong white horse directly in the center of their lines and sent out his commands from there. So, David found himself on the right flank under the command of a young eager captain, part of a shield wall on a huge battlefield, fighting for a land that wasn't his, in a world where he didn't belong, with every chance he would not live to see another day.

He looked around him. Everybody there was fighting for a reason. Whether to keep their freedom, to keep the land on which they worked, to protect their loved ones and families, to keep them from a world in which the queen ruled. He didn't suppose his own quest was much different. He fought to save the woman he loved, to rescue her from imprisonment and the queen's tyranny. He looked up to find the soldier to his right watching him.

"I fight for my family, for my sons!" he said, as if reading David's mind.

"I fight for a woman," replied David.

The soldiers' face split into a grin.

"As good a reason as any!" he said slapping David on the shoulder. He put on his helmet and slid his arm through his shield loop. "Come," he said to David. "It's about time old Albineth was dealt with."

They stepped forward and locked shields with the rest as the order to advance was given. Soon after they began to move the enemy began to close the gap, until bit by bit the enemy became clearer, the features of each soldier became defined, the same grim determination, the same doubts, the same fears. A few strides further and a huge roar went up and the shield walls met with a giant clash.

Afterwards most of the battle was a blur. David remembered feeling like a cog in a huge wheel, push, stab, push, stab, mechanical, unfeeling, moving inexorably onwards, unable to stop for a moment. Eyes filling with sweat, blood everywhere, fallen comrades. He remembered the soldier on his right going down under the blow from an enemy's axe, never to see the family or sons he fought for again. He remembered taking a hit from a huge club, so hard it dented his helmet. He had stood momentarily stunned as another man's axe was raised to finish him off, only for an arrow to appear in the man's left shoulder, freeing his grip on the axe. David glanced behind him quickly and received a salute from Shaeglin as the guide reached for another arrow, before he himself moved forward to close the hole and lock shields with his comrades once again.

Captain Ranzard and his troops had pierced the queens left flank like an arrowhead and when there were few left in front of them to fight, they swept left, carving a huge hole in the left-hand center of the queen's army, as Lord Landstral and his main army cut into them from the front. Although their own left flank hadn't faired so well, they had managed to hold their own, and the queens cause was lost. The acceptance of defeat swept through the enemy army like a wave and in one moment they broke and ran.

Caught up in the battle frenzy some of the allied soldiers gave chase, refusing to let some of the stragglers escape, but some, like David, merely ground to a halt, looking around the once beautiful valley, dazed, struggling to comprehend it was over.

Soldiers started to move among the fallen, looking for brothers, friends, family. Tears of grief mixed with tears of joy as some thought lost in battle were found alive.

David stood in a small gap on the field feeling somewhat removed from the scene surrounding him. He filled his lungs with air once more and checked for injuries. He had a gash on his shield arm where an enemy's sword had glanced high off his shield, but it was nothing serious, his head felt like it was still ringing from the club, and he thought he may have fractured the knuckle of his little finger on his right hand when his sword had been bounced off an enemy's shield. Considering what could have happened, he had got off lightly.

He looked around the battlefield seeking the few faces he did know and spotted Shaeglin. He was helping to carry an injured soldier over to where a group of them lay and were being tended to. The guide stood up and looked over to where David stood. David gave him a sad smile and Shaeglin slowly nodded his head before heading off to help with another soldier.

David heard hooves behind him, and a rider approached leading David's own horse up to him.

"Captain Ranzard said you are to join him," said the soldier passing David the reins. "We ride for the queen's camp."

The camp when they got there was in complete disarray and pretty much empty save for Ranzard and his men. It was around a mile from the battlefield and the queen's army had either grabbed what they could and run, or simply left things there to save themselves. As David approached with the soldier and dismounted, he could see Captain Ranzard questioning a boy of teenage years who was held from running away by one of the captains' men.

"We found him hiding in one of the tents," said Ranzard after greeting David with a firm handshake. "The queen and the remainder of her army are gone."

"Where to?" asked David.

"To Nezure, to the east, back to her castle."

"And her prisoners?"

Ranzard turned to the boy.

"Did she have prisoners here with her before the battle?"

The boy nodded. "A few."

"Anna. Brown hair, green eyes," said David.

"My friend here is looking for a woman." Ranzard explained.

The boy smiled in an act of defiance.

"Well, they're going to be pretty thin on the ground around here, but I can maybe find him one from somewhere..."

The soldier holding him cuffed him hard around the back of the head. Ranzard stepped closer to the boy and put his face level with his to get his full attention.

"This is important, and if you tell us the truth, we will let you go. What happened to the prisoners?"

"The queen took them back to the castle," the boy replied.

"And was there a young woman fitting my friend's description among the prisoners?"

The boy shook his head.

"Can't remember there being. Part of my job was taking food to the prisoners; I can't remember a young woman like that."

"Were all the prisoners here?" Ranzard asked. "Or were there more back at the castle."

"There was a heavy guard left back at the castle, she made sure the town was defended. The prisoners here were generally soldiers captured by groups of her outriders as the army moved across. They were scouts of your own, your own outriders. I should think there are plenty of other prisoners back at the castle, but I wouldn't fancy your chances of getting in there."

Ranzard nodded to his guard.

"Let the boy go," he commanded.

As soon as the grip was released the boy scarpered, darting into the woods behind the camp.

"Will he not warn the queen that we are on our way?" David asked.

"It won't matter. The queens' castle is four days ride from here, she will no doubt expect a pursuit and will have scouts dotted through the landscape to inform her of any approach."

"So, when do we move?" asked David feeling his chances slipping away once more.

"We will have to return to camp first David. I need to speak to Lord Landstral, we may need the army to move again, and I do not control the army."

They found Landstral in his tent, sitting at a desk going through the lists of the dead and the injured. He looked tired, drawn, and older than his fifty something years. David and Ranzard were shown in by a soldier and stood waiting for the lord to look up.

"Yes?" he asked, still running through the lists.

"Captain Ranzard, sir."

Lord Landstral put down the sheets and looked up at the two men.

"Ranzard. Well fought out there today."

"Thank you, sir."

"You lost a few men," he said sadly, glancing back at the lists.

Ranzard lowered his head.

"Too many, sir, yes."

"Well, no doubt we would have lost a lot more without your courage and bravery. I'm truly glad I was on your side!" Lord Landstral said, trying desperately to lighten the moment.

Ranzard gave a wolfish grin.

"I don't think she knew what hit her, sir," he stated.

"Quite," Landstral said rubbing his tired eyes. "Well, thankfully it's over."

"Not quite, sir," said Ranzard.

Landstral stared at him waiting for an explanation.

"The queen has escaped, sir, back to her castle, taking what remains of her army with her."

"Your point being?" the lord asked.

"Surely, we should be finishing the job, sir? Ridding the world of Albineth for good?"

Lord Landstral shook his head.

"Nobody wanted this war, Ranzard, none of us.  This has been simmering quietly for years while each of the land's leaders tried in vain to dissuade Queen Albineth from persevering with her taunts and whatever plans she may have had.  In the end, it came down to this.  When she moved her army into neutral land it was our job to defend our nations.  And that is all, to defend, which we have done."

"But what if she tries again?" asked Ranzard.

"It will take her years to recover from this, and I doubt she could persuade the lords of her own lands to try again after the men they have lost today."  He looked back at his lists.  "I just wish we could have discouraged her without it coming to this.  I'm sorry Ranzard, we have lost too many already."

"But she has prisoners!" exclaimed David.  "You can't leave them there!"

Landstral turned his gaze to David.

"And you are?"

"David…sir," he added.

"Ah, yes, I have heard of you.  You fought bravely today by all accounts.  The prisoners, yes, it is always a concern.  We have prisoners of our own and will be attempting to arrange an exchange, there are those among them that were of importance in her lands."

"And those that aren't important?" asked David bitterly.

"We will do all that we can."

"It will be too late by then," said David turning away.

"Too late for what?" asked Landstral.

"I made this man a promise, sir," said Ranzard stepping forward.  "That if he joined me in battle, I would help to rescue his lady who is held prisoner by the queen.  To stop now, I would be breaking my promise!"

Landstral looked at his lists again.

"Do you know how many eyes I will have to meet whilst I tell them I have failed them?"

Ranzard nodded.

"I know, sir. But the threat remains. Whilst the queen still breathes, she can still inflict pain on people, I for one would have her gone!"

Lord Landstral looked out of the tent, across the battlefield at the men sat around their campfires, talking of their victory, thinking of home. After a few moments he sat back in his chair and looked at Captain Ranzard.

"I cannot order anymore men to their deaths," he put up a hand to stop any interruption. "I cannot order it. The men would have to volunteer. I am sure there are others out there among the campfires who would wish this over for good. The best I can do is to give you clearance, to pursue and detain Queen Albineth. Of course, if you get to the queen and she doesn't wish to be detained," he shrugged. "Things happen in the heat of battle."

Ranzards face split into a grin.

"Thank you, sir!"

"You may not be thankful for it yet," Landstral spoke quietly to the two men's retreating backs, and then called louder out of the tent. "Volunteers mind! The men are free to go home!"

# 10

In the end, they found five hundred soldiers willing to join them.  With Ranzards remaining two hundred that were still fit to travel and fight, it was a small army that set off at first light the following morning on the journey to the queen's castle.  The weather kept changing from a liquid sun to a light drizzle as they rode through an ever-changing landscape of mountain passes and wide valleys.  The mountain passes caused nervousness among the men, as did the roads cutting through dense forest as both gave an opportunity for the enemy to ambush them.  No attack came, although once or twice they spotted lone scouts on the hill tops above the open valleys.  As Ranzard had predicted, the queen would know they were coming.

There was a lightness in the mood of the men as they rode, chatting and joking backwards and forwards, relieving the stress of the battle the day before.  Every soldier there knew they could just as easily be one of the fallen. Ranzard rode alongside David with some of his closest men before and after them as they rode in pairs along the tracks.  The conversation turned from boisterous escapades to families and friends, and then to the woman and loves in their lives.

"This woman that you search for, she must mean a lot to you," said Ranzard loud enough to involve a few of the men in their conversation.

"She does," replied David.  "I've never met anyone like her."

"So, what happened between her and Queen Albineth? Why did she end up a prisoner?"

"I don't know," said David.  He had no intention of telling the soldiers the things that Anna had told him.  "It may have been something from their past.  Anna told me she used to work in the queen's household, that they were friendly once, I guess they fell out. Anna said she's had to move several times to avoid capture."

"How come she got caught this time?" asked the soldier behind him.

"We didn't move quickly enough."

"Sounds to me like she probably ran off with the queen's jewels!" said the soldier laughing.

David pulled on his reins, halting the army behind him, and turned in his saddle to glare at the man behind him.

"There is nothing dishonest about Anna," he said sharply.

The soldier, still chuckling, put up a calming hand.

"Just a joke.  But if you don't know why she was pursued, you have to wonder."

"Maybe he does know," said the soldier's companion. "Maybe he just doesn't want to tell us, maybe he doesn't know who he should trust," he nodded to David, and then he smiled. "If this Anna is as captivating as David says she is, maybe she stole the queen's boyfriend!"

The soldiers surrounding them broke into laughter, as did David.

"Perhaps that's it," said David, deciding to play along. "She was dating one of the queen's guards, he was killed setting Anna free, maybe the queen had been after him herself."

"There you are then!" said Ranzard moving them on again.  "Never spurn a woman in love!" he called to the men's laughter.

David rode in silence for a while after that, trying not to think of what may lie ahead, or what might have happened to Anna, he spent his time studying the landscape around him.  Occasionally as their road took them higher and the ground to their left dropped away for several miles, in the distance he could see snowcapped mountains towards the north, and again he was struck by the beauty of this world.

"Penny for your thoughts?" said Ranzard who had been watching him on and off for a while.

"I was actually just enjoying the beauty of this place."
Ranzard nodded.

"It's hard to believe the battle really happened yesterday when you're riding through such peaceful landscape today, hopefully it will do the men some good.  A couple of days of this will hopefully give them a respite before the challenges that lay ahead."

"Have you ever been to the north?" asked David, still looking across to the snowcapped peaks.

"A couple of times," replied Ranzard. "It's good hunting country, it's wild.  Now and then, small parties venture there from our lands, just to keep some form of contact and check what they are doing, just in case they decide to band together and seek more land.  They never do, they are peaceful enough, the tribes have some skirmishes between themselves from time to time, but it never spills over past the mountain passes and elsewhere.  But they are hard, they have to be to survive up there, and you must respect them, they hold no allegiance to anyone but themselves.  They have no fear of us, and no particular interest."

"They sound interesting," said David, thinking for the first time in a while of his cottage on its own out in the forest.

"Some of their women are beautiful," said the soldier in front of them hearing their conversation.  "Cosgar!" he called to an old soldier a couple of riders in front of him. "Weren't you married to a woman from the north?!"

"I was!" the old soldier called back.

"And was she beautiful?!"

"Aye she was!" said the old soldier.  "And as cold as those snowcapped mountains!"

The laughter rippled through the riders and once again the conversation turned more raucous, occasionally turning to song as a few of the men took turns singing songs from home and songs from the taverns. As they continued their journey, they would still spot riders keeping tabs on their progress, reminding them of their task and the purpose of their travel. When they stopped for the night, it was a heavy guard that Ranzard set up around their camp. He had no intention of failing before they even got there.

They made good progress. It was mid-morning on the fourth day when the road wound down from the last mountain pass and brought them into a large open valley. Towards the far end of the valley on a rise of ground about two miles from them they got their first view of Nezure castle, the queen's stronghold. On the low ground below the castle were groups of houses and small holdings outside of the city walls, and between these and the soldiers were farms, larger tracts of land used to grow crops to feed the city. The city itself was big, sat snug and secure behind a tall defensive wall on its outcrop. From where they were it looked impregnable, and David wondered not for the first time about the sanity of trying to storm a city with such a small army.

"What happens now then?" David asked, turning to Captain Ranzard. "We just ride right up to the gates and demand the queen submits?"

"Pretty much," said Ranzard. "Hopefully they will let us in to speak to her at least, we could do with getting a look at the place."

"Are you mad? From what I've heard of her so far, she's likely to just send her army out and eradicate us."

"What's left of her army."

"True, they were pretty scattered when we last saw them," David conceded.

Ranzard looked across at David.

"I must stick to my orders. I must give the queen the opportunity to come quietly. She will refuse of course, and when she does..." he shrugged.

David looked from him back to the castle on its hill and wondered how Ranzard planned to storm it.

As they rode on, the farmland gradually started to disappear and be replaced by houses, at first, they were small poorly built things out of wood or mud and straw. Gradually these were replaced by stone and brick-built houses that increased in size and splendor as they got closer to the castle. They had barely seen anyone as they rode down the street, the people of the town choosing to stay safe in their houses or possibly retreating inside the castle walls.

A little way from the castle the streets of houses stopped and opened onto a large level field of shortly grazed grass. The track continued, splitting through the middle of the field toward the hill and up to the castle gates. In front of the gates and in a line on either side were around fifty of the queen's soldiers. In the middle of the line, next to her flagbearer was the queen.

Ranzard signaled to his men to fan out across the field in lines and to wait there as twenty of his soldiers, including David, headed across the field and approached the queen. They rode in an arrowhead formation with the six soldiers in the middle riding right up to the queen in the center of her line, and the rest of the soldiers halting in a staggered line outward behind them.

"Your majesty," Ranzard bowed in his saddle in front of the queen.

"Captain Ranzard," she replied nodding briefly to him. She glanced sideways at David, and to the other soldiers flanking out behind them, and then past them at the small army at their backs across the short field.

"To what do I owe this pleasure? Come to check I am safely home?" she said, her focus back on the captain.

"Not exactly your majesty.  Although it is good to know where the enemy lies, a few good scouts could have brought me that information."

"Then why do you trespass on my lands?" the queen asked harshly.

"Your lands," muttered Ranzard smiling, he looked at the ground as if deep in thought.  "You intend to hold onto them then?  Even having lost…to the victor go the spoils?  Are we to believe that if you had won you would have withdrawn your army back here and let the world carry on untouched?"

"Just because I have lost a battle does not mean I have lost the war!" shouted the queen.

Ranzard turned in his saddle to gaze back at his small army and then turned back expressionless to look at the queen and across the rest of her soldiers.

"No, quite," he said quietly nodding.  "Not the war, no."

The queen bristled at that, as did several of her officers, half expecting a signal and a sudden rush of soldiers.  When one did not come, the queen frowned at the captain.

"So, what is it you want?  What are you here for?"

"I have been ordered by the rulers of the west and the south to arrest Queen Albineth, to assure peace across our world."

"To arrest…?"  The queen started to form words that didn't come, and then just laughed.  "What makes you think we would just come quietly?"

"We?" Ranzard shook his head.  "My orders are for the queen only; I have no orders for the arrest of anyone else."

A few of her soldiers exchanged quick glances.

"To arrest me on what grounds, what charges?"

"For the breaking of the treaty," the captain replied quietly and levelly, all humor gone from him.

"Treaty!" the queen spluttered.  "That treaty was signed years ago by cowards!  Generation after generation has passed since then!  You can't tell me people still take that seriously!  Those pompous fools in the west certainly don't, since when have they stuck to the rules?  I didn't sign any treaty!"

"You agreed to the treaty when you became queen," Ranzard said patiently.  "It is automatic when you take the crown, the promises are understood."

"Promises!  What is the point of ruling the land if you inherit promises that hamstring you against making changes to the governing of your own land!  How are you ever meant to rule?"

"And what of the promises to your own people?" asked Ranzard.

The queen took a tighter grip on her reins as her horse started to jink, sensing the tension of its rider.

"Don't assume you know anything about kingdoms, Captain!" she spat the word as an insult.  "I was ruling this land when you were still being bounced on your daddy's knee!  Upstart!  I could have you shot on the spot!"

"I don't doubt it."

"As we speak there are trained archers with enough arrows pointed at you and your little party here to turn you all into hedgehogs."

Ranzard smiled and looked above him at the castle walls. Sunlight glinted off enough arrowheads to back up her claims, but he kept his smile in place as he lowered his gaze back to the queen.

"But would you make it back in time?" he asked her, still smiling.

She looked past him at five hundred soldiers across a short field.  They were not relaxed, each man still had hold of his reins, each man ready to charge.  There was no talking going on, no banter between the soldiers.  Her eyes returned to the captain.

"Then it seems we have reached a stale mate Captain," she said.

"It would appear so," he said nodding. "I can wait until the morning for your answer if you wish for time to consider."

"The answer would be the same Captain. Go home. You do not have enough men with you to storm this castle and you know it. If one of those horses start to move across this field shaft after shaft will rain down on you and your men. Go home. Meet with your elders if you wish, see if they will join you and bring their army," she chuckled as she started to turn her horse back toward the castle. "Didn't want to come did they?" she called over her shoulder. "Fruitless chase! And all that. I admire your youthful optimism Captain Ranzard but return home." She nudged her horse into a canter, her soldiers following her in a line back toward the castle gates.

# 11

"What happens now then?" asked David as they returned to the rest of the men.

"Now, we set up camp for the night." Ranzard replied.

"This close to the castle?!" David looked across the field to the imposing grey walls. "You plan to have your army sleep on her doorstep? Isn't that inviting trouble?"

Ranzard smiled.

"I don't believe I said anything about sleeping, although it may not be a bad idea for the men to catch up in shifts between now and night fall, for it's going to be a long night."

"You don't plan to try to storm those walls?"

"The walls? No, there's no way over them."

"Instead of talking in riddles would you like to tell me what you do have planned, as I assume you do have a plan and you're not just a mad man? Don't forget, my sole purpose for being here is to my knowledge still inside that castle. If not over the walls, then how?"

"Straight through the gate, or one of the gates anyway, not necessarily the front one."

David looked back at the castle and stood shaking his head. He admired the man's courage but the moment they started with battering rams he could envisage the fire and fury that would be unleashed from those within. Leaving there alive, and alive with Anna, was once again looking a remote hope.

Ranzard left him to his thoughts for a moment and then reached out an arm and gripped David's shoulder.

"None of this is going to be easy David, but don't misunderstand my confidence for complacency. I am not the headstrong youth that people have me down as, although I may have helped that thought along the way, it doesn't hurt for people to underestimate me.  If people think they have me sussed, they won't bother to look closer at what else may be going on.  The queen thinks she has me beaten.  Even a headstrong youth wouldn't be stupid enough to charge straight at that castle with five hundred men, it would be suicide.  I know that and she knows that.  But there are other things that she doesn't know, other things that I have been planning and setting up for years.  This was coming a long time ago, the leaders of the other lands were hoping talks would suffice, that peace could be found with the queen, but I always knew it would come down to war.  The best way to win any strategic game is to have an idea of what you are doing several moves ahead.  I don't like to leave a job half done.  Rest assured, a gate will open tonight, and the job will be finished."

"But I still don't get how you are going to get in unnoticed."

"I'm sure they will notice us soon enough, it is going to be one hell of a fight David, we will not all come out of this alive.  But remember the queen is a tyrant, not all the people inside the queen's city love their queen."

David stood on the parapet watching the scene below him as he gained his breath and steadied his nerves.  It had all gone smoothly, it had all gone to plan, and still they had already lost around one third of their men.

After his conversation with David, Captain Ranzard had called all his troops' leaders in to explain his plans in full.  For years there had been people leaving the city to search for a better life elsewhere, and over the years Ranzard had recruited some of those worst affected by the queen and had sent them back in to live among their people and wait for this day.  Some had been trained as spies, some had been trained as assassins, all had been trained in combat.  When the signal was given, all those who had waited for years for this moment rose up, it was like a bomb going off in the city's midst. All eyes of the queen's guards had been trained outwards at the threat from without, expecting a futile assault on the city's walls and outer defenses. The uprising from within caught the city's troops off balance and the initial effect was brutal. As the city's guards finally got themselves in order and turned to deal with the sudden threat from within, Ranzards troops advanced on the city, heading to the south gate where some of Ranzards spies on the inside had been deployed to open the gates from within. As the city's guards were just managing to turn the tide inside back in their favor, another five hundred trained soldiers came pouring in through the south gate and the outer defenses of the city crumbled.

David had been sent with one hundred soldiers to turn left as they entered the city and find the staircase to the parapets along that side. They were to clear all higher defenses so the main army could not be fired upon in the main space below. It had been mayhem. The uprising had already made it up through there in places, spilling upwards for the very same reason, to smother the threat from above. There were pockets of them still fighting with city guards, and though the city guards were starting to gain the upper hand, David and his men cleared each threat as they passed through, adding members of the uprising to his numbers just as they lost members of their troops. Eventually they cleared all the upper defenses and had a moments respite to organize themselves and take stock of the battle below.

David leaned against the wall behind him, sucking in air and letting the adrenalin settle. The scene below him looked much the same as the scene around him and the other levels he had passed through. Those of the queen's guards who had been willing to submit had for now been bound, those who had continued to fight had been badly wounded or killed. Their bodies lay littered with those of Ranzards men who had failed to make it through. There were no celebrations, other than each man's personal relief that they were still alive. Any celebrations would have been premature as the battle continued at the open gate through the second line of defenses that led to the queen's castle. As David's gaze wandered around the carnage of the main space below, he caught sight of Ranzard looking backwards and forwards along the line of upper defenses and David raised his sword to gain the captain's attention. Ranzard spotted the move and signaled to David to join him back at ground level and David gathered his troops and made the descent.

"The first part is won," said Ranzard as David approached. "We managed to get enough soldiers into the second gateway before they could close it as they were retreating but we now need to join them and break through. It's a hard place to fight within that limited space and our losses there have been heavy, those still left there fighting will need to be replaced and rested. I would like to lead this final charge and have you and your men behind me, when we push through to the castle square we can fan out and give one final onslaught. I have men posted at each gate, the queen doesn't leave here, understood?"

David nodded and he and his men followed Ranzards troops in through the gate. The losses had indeed been grave, and David thought of all those brave men fighting and falling to gain each few foot. They left a space on their right-hand side through which the spent men in front could retreat and then they pushed on through. The queen's troops had been equally brave, but they buckled under the fresh onslaught. Ranzard and David and their men spilled out into the courtyard just as the queen and her bodyguard were backing up to the castle. Albineth's bodyguards were made up of twenty of her strongest, most loyal soldiers, and as five entered the building with the queen, fifteen of the others split off to guard the door to buy some time, but time for what David wasn't sure. Thoughts of Anna flooded his mind, thoughts that she may be in there and that maybe where the queen was heading. With one guttural cry he sprang forward, sprinting across the courtyard followed a short distance behind by several of his alarmed soldiers. Halfway across he heard a shout from Ranzard but whether a call to retreat or a signal for his men to follow David never heard or cared. All the frustration and worry had turned to blind rage, and nothing was going to stop him. The closest few of David's men had caught up with him as David closed the final gap and launched himself at the queen's guards. They were highly trained men, but they weren't prepared for this snarling mad man and the first guard in his way fell under a wild blow that all the training in the world wouldn't have stopped. The rest subtly edged to the side to look for a more controlled opponent and they left a small gap that David quickly shot through and continued helter-skelter through the open doorway. When Ranzard finally caught up with David he found David in one of the queen's rooms hunting around in frustration.

"That was extremely brave out there David but not exactly as I had ordered. What exactly are you looking for?" he added as David ignored his first comment and continued to search.

"They are holed up in that room!" David snapped, and then remembered who he was speaking to. "I need something to break the door open with, sir."

Ranzard nodded and signaled to a couple of his men who had entered the room with him.

"Get that large oak trunk from the room we just passed through, and we will try it with that. If that fails, we will call for some axes."

The axes weren't needed, the room made up part of the queen's personal chambers and had not been built as a fortification. Nobody could have ever believed a small army would get through the double walls outside. The oak trunk with four men using it as a battering ram soon broke the clasp and lock and loosened one of the hinges at the same time. Ranzard wasn't going to be usurped again and quickly entered the room first closely followed by David, but as David entered behind the captain, he felt Ranzard falter in front of him and push back against David. As they retreated into the room David could see an arrow protruding from Ranzards right shoulder. Although high and not mortal he wouldn't be using a sword anymore today.

"Shields men!" Ranzard ordered. "That was rather foolish of me," he said to David as his men retrieved their shields. The captain looked at the floor and let out a long sigh then raised his head again to stare at David with a wolfish smile. "Time to go get her David."

Ranzard had one of his men pull the arrow from his shoulder and picked up his shield in his left hand. He once again took the lead to deflect any other arrows that may be waiting for them as they advanced into the room.

At such close quarters the fighting was messy. The room itself was quite large but scattered furniture made it impossible for much order. Ranzard deflected several arrows with his shield before another wild shot caught him in the side of the leg and sent him momentarily to the floor. They lost both of Ranzards men in the final skirmish, but they took four of the queen's guards with them, leaving the guard with the bow at the back of the room standing in front of the queen. As the guard reached for another arrow David looked for something to throw, finding nothing but his sword, in one last ditch attempt he hurled it toward the guard. The guard was notching his arrow and seeing the movement in the corner of his eye automatically edged to his side to avoid the object. In doing so the sword continued straight on and hit the queen who had been blind-sided by the guard in front of her. It hit her low in the torso below her ribcage. Stunned at his inability to save his queen the guard stood momentarily transfixed. David wasted no time, charging at the guard he sent him sprawling to the floor and finding a heavy earthenware jug within his reach brought it smashing down onto the head of the guard, knocking him unconscious. Raising himself from the floor, David went over to the back of the room where the queen sat with her back propped against the wall, blood on her hands, a look of disbelief on her face, as she lived out her final moments.

"Where is she?" David demanded standing over her.

Albineth looked up frowning at David, reaching out her hands to show him the blood, as if he wasn't aware of it.

"Where is she?" he repeated.

"What? Where is who?" Queen Albineth asked, not understanding.

"Anna! Where is Anna?!"

The queen looked a moment at David, then at the blood on her hands and then at the sword in her side. When she looked back at David a dark cloud of anger had crossed her gaze.

"You!" she spat. "You who killed one of my best captains, who killed my soldiers in the woods, and now…" she raised her hands again, gesturing towards her wound.

"To be fair," said David calmly. "I had help in the woods, and your captain was an accident, and if you yourself hadn't sent them after innocent people in the first place then none of this would have happened."

"Innocent!" Albineth tried to laugh but it ended in a wince of pain. "Innocent. Far from it. Anna was keeping secrets from me."

"Anna didn't know her secret."

"She knew."

"She did not. She tried to tell you that, you didn't listen. Now where is she?"

The queen stayed silent for a moment, letting a wave of fresh pain crash through her before raising her head once more to smile sweetly at David.

"Somewhere you will never find her. Somewhere nobody will ever find her."

David felt a cold web of fear spread through him.

"Did you think she was in the castle?" the queen asked wincing through more pain. "At the camp at the battlefield maybe? All you had to do was storm through the defenses and win back the lady? This isn't a fairytale! You don't stay queen this long without preparing."

"What have you done? Where is she?!"

"To the north. In the northlands. On a cold windswept plateau, in a cold dark cave, with enough food to last her until I came back for her, and no more."

"Tell me where!" David pleaded.

The queen shook her head.

"I knew somebody was looking for her, I thought it could turn out to be important, so I hid her."

"But it doesn't matter now," said David. "You gain nothing by keeping it a secret."

"I gain nothing by telling either," replied the queen. "She was to be my bargaining piece. If I won the war she wouldn't be needed, I could let her go, or in the euphoria of winning maybe I would've just forgotten she was there," the queen shrugged. "If I lost the battle and was captured, I could trade her, my life for hers." She looked down at her wound. "My life. You struck a bad bargain."

David searched his mind for a reason for her to tell him but could find none. There was no appealing to a conscience that didn't exist.

"I am dying," stated the queen. "And now so is Anna. Her secrets will die with her, and mine with me."

"Secrets?" asked David.

"Everybody has secrets, David, even you. Do you think you just stumbled into our world? That's a regular occurrence in your world is it, people just wandering off?"

David frowned at her.

"I know a few things. I maybe know a few more things than you," the queen said in a rasping breath. "And do you know what?"

“What?” asked David.
“I’m not going to tell you.”

# 12

They had been her last words.  Her parting statement had been a parting shot, and it hit David hard.  It was over.  He slumped back against the turned over cupboard that lay opposite the queen and finally let the last few days of exhausting conflict wash over him.  He felt like he didn't have an ounce of energy left, and so just sat there staring at the dead body of the queen as he heard the room gradually filling with Ranzards soldiers.

He heard shuffled footsteps approaching and felt a hand placed on his shoulder and the captain's voice low and level in his ear.

"Did you find out David?  Do you know where Anna is?"

David shook his head numbly as unconsciousness finally took him.

"I think he's back again," said Jeannie.

"How bad is it this time?" asked Tim.

"Not sure, bit black and blue.  Got quite a shiner on his left eye.  Can you hear me, David?" Jeannie paused. "He's still circling the airport, I think.  He's got a gash on his right shoulder that might need stitches, I don't know.  The rest of him is possibly ok."

David winced as Jeannie checked around his torso.

"It's possible he's cracked a rib or two, maybe just badly bruised.  David?  David, what happened this time?"

"War." It was spoken quietly but heard by both. Jeannie turned to give Tim a worried look.  Tim stepped forward and leaned down towards the sofa.

"Did you find her David?"

"No."

Darkness once again took him, but this time it was a neutral darkness, not really in either world. Through all the physical brutality of the battle and all the searching and riding it was his mind, his resolve that had truly been pushed to its limits, and both needed a respite. It was several hours later when he came to again, his friends were still there, still watching over him. As he propped himself up against the arm of the chair Jeannie passed him a cup of sweetened tea.

"Are you alright David?" she asked. "You look quite beaten up."

David nodded. "There are no wounds really troubling me. I've never been in a battle before, no amount of novels can prepare you for the reality of that, it was horrendous."

"Did you win?" Tim asked.

David nodded. "But so many men are gone forever. There was a huge battle, the queen's army finally crumpled, and she was pushed back to her castle. Our captain and five hundred others pursued her there and stormed the castle at night. It's over, well and truly over."

It was said with such finality that Jeannie looked sadly at Tim. David didn't look like a winner, he looked exhausted, defeated, and Jeannie dreaded the answer to her next question.

"Did you get any information as to where Anna might be?"

"Yes. But it's of no use. She is in the northern wilderness. From what I can gather it is an area the size of Scotland, maybe twice that size and more remote, a cold mountainous region and I would be searching it on horseback. The queen told me she left Anna there with enough food for a limited time only, that time is quickly diminishing."

"Is there no way of forcing her to tell you where?" asked Tim.

"No, not now I've killed her."

Tim frowned at Jeannie. "Dear God."

"Her guard was about to shoot an arrow at me, I threw my sword at him, he moved, and it hit the queen. I didn't want her dead, I wanted answers, now I have nothing."

They sat in silence for a while, each of them deep in thought, trying hard to think of a solution.

"I'll have to try to get back there," said David, thinking aloud. "But for what purpose, I'm not sure. It feels like it's over, but I can't accept it's over. You can't just stop trying, can you? Until you know for sure?"

"It could take years David," said Jeannie. "All that time away from this world, there's no telling what that might do to you."

"But I can't just give up, can I?! She is out there somewhere, cold, starving," he shook his head in frustration.

"I've been thinking," said Tim. "All through last night and again while you've been talking. There may be something that we've not considered. I need to ask you a few questions, David, if you can bear with me a moment?"

David nodded. "I'm not going anywhere just yet."

"The first thing is, when you are in the otherworld, when you have been there for some time and are living your life in that world, do you stop thinking of this one? Have you ever got so involved there that any thoughts of this cottage, your artwork, your life here have slipped your mind completely for any considerable length of time?"

David thought back to his time in Selaster, when things were peaceful, his simple work there and his time with Anna.

"Yes," he replied. "There was a time I remember I hadn't thought about here for several weeks, it had slipped my mind entirely."

Jeannie groaned.

"Sorry," said David. "It's not that you're not important to me too."

"It's not that," Jeannie replied. "I'm worried David, if you go off searching again that you won't return. That this," she tapped the side of her head, "won't return."

Tim placed a hand on her arm.

"It's ok, Jeannie," he turned again to David. "David, when you are in that world, time travels much faster than in this, yes? To no set time difference but you can spend months in that world and merely hours have passed in this?"

"Yes, that's true. It varies, but it does move quicker there."

Tim nodded. "And this queen, she was pursuing Anna because she thought Anna held a secret to eternal youth?"

"That's right," said David. "Anna wasn't appearing to age."

"And Anna's memory of her childhood was vague?"

"She never spoke of it."

"And when you are in that world your physical presence remains in this? Or should I say, it would appear you have a physical presence in both worlds, that although your mind is gone from this world your body does not disappear? While we have been waiting for you to come back, you have, physically at least, remained on that sofa."

"Well, you would know that better than me, but yes, I'm not a ghost in that world, and if you say I remain here the whole time then that must be the case."

"And when you wake in this world it is as if you have been in suspended animation, you don't wake up excessively hungry or thirsty? It's like your physical form here has merely been put on hold?"

"That's right, yes. The more you say, the weirder it sounds. But what are you getting at?"

Tim leaned forward.

"David. Has it occurred to you that Anna, like you, could be from this world?"

Jeannie turned to look at Tim. David was staring through him weighing up everything that had just been said.

"It's possible I suppose," David replied. "I'd not considered it. Anna spoke of twenty years or more there."

"Indeed," said Tim. "But that possibly would only equate to a few months here."

"But somebody would miss her, surely," said Jeannie. "Somebody would turn up at her house looking for her."

"Depends on her situation," Tim shrugged. "If David didn't have you checking on him how long could he go unnoticed all the way out here?"

David nodded. "I see your point. But I don't see how it helps us, it just means as well as being on some random windswept hillside there she could also be in some random house in some random town here. That could prove even more of a needle in a haystack."

"I agree it could. It could be completely hopeless, but there was one thing that I thought might give us an edge, might narrow the search, but I need this morning and we need to leave here and go to my shop."

"Why?" asked David.

"Because I need to search through my sales information, and I possibly need to search the internet." Tim looked at their blank faces. "Sorry, let me explain. I am assuming that she entered that world the same way you did, via that music. If she didn't then we are done for, she will be lost without a trace, so that's all we have got to go on. If she did enter via that music, it narrows it down considerably because that cd is very rare. Rare to the point that I don't know where it exists outside of my shop. You see, I get people come into the shop with boxes of CDs to sell to me for whatever they can get, and I then price them up individually and sell them on, that's my business. Lots of people are getting rid of their collections and listening to their music online now, but there are still those who like to own the physical copy, so I become the middleman in the cycle. Anyway, that cd was brought in in a box with several copies of the same by an old man who was having a clear out.  Afterwards, when I tried to trace the origins of it and what price copies were being sold for elsewhere, I could find no other copies.  Sometimes people bring in copies of music they've had a hand in themselves, old band CDs etc.  Leftovers that they never sold at gigs.  Some aren't that great, some, like this one, are very good, so I priced it up and thought no more about it.  There were only a dozen copies in that box, David has one, I have the other copy he returned to me and two others, that means I've sold eight.  Some across the counter sales will be hard to trace, I don't take contact details of everybody who just pops in to buy something in the shop, but some of those sales may have been online and I will have postal addresses for them.  It's a long shot, but I think it's worth a try."

David had already left the sofa and was putting on his coat and shoes.

"It's more of a lead than we're going to get from a dead queen," he said as he walked out the door.

# 13

David had been pacing the floor of the shop for several minutes.  He wondered if this was such a good idea after all, every minute lost in this world was substantially longer there and he had no idea how much longer Anna had.  He knew she was in that world; he had no idea if she was in this one and he couldn't help but feel that he should be riding like the devil possessed scouring the bleak north country rather than hanging around in a record shop looking through old receipts.  Although what his friend said made sense, it felt too inactive, and so he paced, just to be doing something.

"Did Anna ever give you a surname?" Tim broke into his thoughts.

David was next to him in a flash.

"You've found something?"

"Possibly.  Did she give you a surname?"

"No.  What have you found?"

"Eight discs sold.  Five online, three across the counter with no trace.  Of the five, there are two possibilities.  There is Anna Sterling who lives in Devon, and there is an Anna Humphries who lives in Inverness, Scotland."

"Devon's closest," said David, grabbing his coat from off the peg.

"Hold on," said Tim.  "I have something else I want to check first, if we go all the way down to Devon and it turns out to be the one in Inverness, we could have wasted a lot of precious time."

"True, but we are also wasting time just sitting here."

"Hold on," Tim repeated.  "I just want to check if there are any reviews, I can't believe I didn't do this sooner!  I ask people to leave online reviews on the music I sell in my shop, it helps for future sales and helps me to see what's well received, especially with the obscure stuff.  Bingo! There's a review here that looks like it…"

"What?  What is it?" asked David.

"My God."

"What?!"

"Listen to this review. "" I ordered this online as I've not been sleeping well, and I thought it might help me.  The music is beautiful, and very hypnotic, but is ruined somewhat at the end by the sound of hurried footsteps…"""

"So, which one was it?!"  asked David exasperated.

Tim turned in his seat still looking amazed.

"We head to Devon." He said.


All the way to Devon Tim and Jeannie had tried to settle David's excitement.  Trying hopelessly to tell him this may not necessarily be the same Anna, but David was having none of it.  After all the disappointment, the bleakness of thinking she was lost forever, this was the only ray of light he had, and he clung to it.  If he could find her, if he could bring her back to this world, all would be ok.

They drove for a few hours and eventually came to the village in the north of Devon.  A small main square of houses and a couple of shops sat in the deep cut of a valley surrounded by a spread of other houses and small farmsteads that spread bit by bit up the slopes of the surrounding hills.  Tim went to the newsagents and asked directions, and they followed the zigzag of winding roads that led them out of the main square and up the west side of the valley.  Eventually they found a track road that took them past two cottages and then headed further through a small wood.  As they neared the wood, they came across an old lady braving the rain in her waterproofs to walk her dog. She had just left the woodland path and waited by the side of the road for their car to pass. Although the surroundings matched the directions they had been given, out of politeness they stopped to ask the old lady.

"Hello," said David after winding down his window. "Not a nice day to be walking your dog."

"It's not so nice," said the old lady smiling. ""But I don't mind, and neither does the dog."

"Is this the way to Rose Cottage?" he asked.

"It is," she said. "Are you friends of theirs?" she was studying them a little.

"I'm a friend of Anna's," said David. "I've not seen her for a while, I've been getting a bit concerned. Is it ok to go up do you think?"

The lady nodded relaxing a little. "You're ok to head up there, it's nothing to do with me, I live in one of the cottages you just passed, so I know them well. But I don't think you'll find anybody there. Nobody has seen Anna for a few months. The last time I saw her she mentioned she was going travelling, the place has been locked up for months, curtains drawn. I've looked after the garden a bit, keeping the weeds down, I don't know when she'll be back. She deserves a bit of life, bless her, after looking after her father for so long, putting her own life on hold, not good for one so young."

"Did she say where she was travelling to?" asked David, fearing another dead end.

The old lady shook her head. "She mentioned it is all. After her father passed, what, five months ago now I guess, he left her a good bit of money and the cottage is paid for, so why not?" she nodded up the track. "Anna gave up her job at the little bookstore and said she might go off and do a bit of travelling. I've not seen her since, so she must have headed off I guess."

"So, you didn't see her leave then? asked David.

"No," the lady frowned a little. "But the place looks deserted, and she'd mentioned to others hereabouts of her plans."

"Oh well, I guess she'll be back at some point," said David to reassure her.

"I'm sure she will," the old lady smiled. "Maybe you can spot a clue as to where she's gone."

"Maybe," said David cheerfully. "Thank you for your time," he added as Tim pulled away to follow the track up through the woods.

Rose cottage was a small dwelling on its own in a clearing just beyond the wood. There were a few fields of open farmland sloping down to the south, allowing a view down through part of the valley. It was a beautiful little place, and it did look and feel deserted. David knocked on the door and tried to look through the windows but couldn't see through any gaps to the inside.

"She may not be here David, maybe she did go travelling and took the music with her," Jeannie said.

David looked at her blankly for a second and then picked up a small rock from the edge of one of the rose beds and headed around to the back of the house.

"Only one way to find out," he called over his shoulder.

Jeannie and Tim followed quickly behind.

"David, you can't just…" said Jeannie too late.

David hefted the rock and smashed it several times into the large kitchen window, using the rock after the pane had gone to chip away the fragmented glass around the edges. Once the lower sill was clear of sharp shards David climbed up through the window and turned to give a hand to the other two.

"I don't have time to mess around," he said.

"No, no I can see that," said Jeannie as she was helped through the window.

"If anybody asks, I'll just tell them I was concerned she was still in here. Besides, I can pay for a new window."

Jeannie took his hand and climbed in followed by Tim. They left the kitchen and crossed the small hallway into the sitting room. It was a relatively small room with a couple of armchairs by the window, a television cabinet in the corner, and by the back of the wall, a sofa. On the sofa lay a young woman, beautiful, thin, pale, Anna. The room was cold, the whole cottage was unnaturally cold for the time of year, but not, David guessed, as cold as the cave she was in in Larquolyn. He rushed to her side trying to wake her, shaking her gently at first and then with a little more force.

"Anna," he called to her. "Anna, wake up. It's David! You're alright. Anna!" He took her hand, squeezing it and then rubbing them to try to warm them, they were as cold as stone. He turned to the other two, looking desperately at them. Tim looked at Jeannie and shrugged, then headed off looking for blankets.

"Maybe if we get her warm Jeannie," he called to her as she set off searching around the cottage. "See if you can get the heating on."

Anna was cold, painfully cold. Her food had run out three days ago, and she had been rationing it before then. The water had run out yesterday and the temperature had dropped again last night. She was drifting, drifting away. She was dying, slowly, and she knew it. She lay huddled in the cave in her bonds, shackled. In her hands she held the small carving of a horse that David had made her and that she had carried about her person ever since. Her thoughts kept straying back to their time together, it was a comfort at least. If she allowed herself to drift, to dream, she could see him, she could hear his voice calling her name.

David knelt with his head buried in the side of the sofa. He didn't know whether to cry or to scream out in anger. To have got so close, to have found her but in the wrong world, to have still lost her was soul destroying. Maybe if he listened to her music, here in her cottage, maybe that would take him straight to her. Maybe while he was next to her in this world, while he was so close, while he was holding her hand. Her hand. There was something in it, there was something held between her hand and his. He moved his fingers around feeling for the object, something small, wooden, it was the horse carving he had given her.

"David," Jeannie said. "David? I think she maybe waking up."

David raised his head, he looked at his hand which now held the small carving and then slowly he looked up into the eyes of Anna. Wide eyes, scared eyes.

"David?" Anna questioned.

She was frowning at him, unsure. She looked beyond him to the two strangers and then passed them at the now unfamiliar objects in the room. At the room itself, the cottage she had left three months ago, twenty years ago. Her eyes returned to him again.

"David?" she asked again.

David nodded, smiling.

"It's me Anna, it's ok. Queen Albineth is dead, you're safe, you're home."

"David." This time a statement. The relief of seeing him again finally outweighed all her current fears and she threw her arms around him in a hard embrace as the tears finally flowed.

David explained everything to Anna as she sat quietly in her cottage sipping the hot chocolate Jeannie had found in the kitchen cupboard. The memories of her life here in Devon slowly returned to her. She had lost her mum when she was young and had grown up in the cottage with her father. When he was diagnosed with cancer she had helped to look after him until his death earlier that year. Anna had planned to travel soon after and had quit her job to clear her head and decide where to go, but she hadn't been sleeping well and was having trouble making her choices. She had shopped online for some music to try to help her relax and to sleep and had ordered the same CD that Jeannie had given to David. Like him, she had heard footsteps on the disc and the noise had pulled her into the otherworld. The footsteps for her had been the young guard that she had formed a friendship with before he was killed.

David stayed in Devon for a few days as Jeannie and Tim returned home. David and Anna discussed what they were going to do, and Anna decided that as she felt she still needed to leave the cottage, at least for a while, she would return with David to the New Forest.

And so, after all their strange travels, their fights and battles, they returned to a quiet normality in David's cottage in the woods.

# EPILOGUE

The days gently rolled on, the daily routines slowly returned, and the security and warmth of the cottage gradually worked its magic. Anna eventually started to feel a part of this world again and memories of her time here before entering the otherworld drifted back and all the pieces slowly fell into place. The quietness of the glade and the humble, simple living helped as it was not so far removed from the day-to-day chores of life spent in the otherworld. David encouraged her to change things and turn the cottage into her home. Things were rearranged, tidied, and packed away.

On a clear through some of the old clothes one day she found David's old jacket, the one he had been wearing the day he was attacked by the rock bear, and she took the ruined jacket out to the bins. The jacket had not been worn since that desperate scrabble for safety and caught inside the collar was a driftberry. As she walked down the few steps from the cottage to the garden the berry was released from the fold of cloth and tumbled to the ground, unseen by Anna. Unseen by Anna but noticed by a blackbird who sat in one of the trees by the edge of the glade. As Anna turned the corner towards the side of the cottage the blackbird swooped down and picked up the berry. He flew onwards and onwards with his prize, deep into the woodland, until finally he found a perch by a small glade far from human footsteps. There he pecked into the berry, and deciding that it hadn't been worth it after all, he discarded it, dropping it onto the forest floor and flying away.

The seasons rolled by, and the berry perished, slowly rotting into the ground on which it had fallen until all that was left was a tiny seed. The seasons changed and the leaves fell, falling onto the seed and the surrounding ground.  Winters cold came and went, followed by the rains and the warm spring sunshine, and slowly but surely the seed germinated and grew.  As the years passed the driftberry grew into a strong parent plant, spreading fresh berries onto the forest floor around it, until there became, in that small remote glade, in a place where people seldom trod, a small copse of driftberries.

If you happened to be somebody who could step from this world to the otherworld and travel through the many places in both worlds, you may have noticed that this little copse of driftberries was almost identical to a small copse of driftberries outside of a small town on the edge of a forest in the otherworld.

And had you been sitting there one day on the edge of the forest in the otherworld you may have seen a young girl enter the woods.  A young girl who was told to stay out of the forest and not to go wandering there on her own.

And had you been sitting there; you would have seen the girl wander up to the little copse of driftberries and vanish.